THE WORST PIRATE HUNTERS IN THE FRINGE

Book Three, Dumb Luck and Dead Heroes

Skyler Ramirez

Persephone Entertainment Inc.

Print ISBN: 9798870629667

Printed in the United States of America

Published by Persephone Entertainment Inc.
Texas, USA

To my parents, who encouraged and fed my love of reading in my youth. And for being so patient with me, even when they caught me crouched down and reading by my younger brother's night light when it was way past my bedtime.

CONTENTS

CHAPTER 1

Interrogated by an Idiot

"**M**r. Mendoza, you may be the dumbest man I've ever met."

You ever have one of those days when the hits just keep on coming? Seriously, I thought that day for me was just two days ago when Owen Thompson hijacked my ship and put an explosive implant into my XO's neck. But today is quickly inserting itself for the title of 'Worst Day Ever'. Or maybe it's just an all-around crappy week.

There we were, minding our own business, trying to get out of the Fiori system as quickly as we could while avoiding any official entanglements, when the mother of all official entanglements sought *us* out. I was rudely awakened from a nice nap, my ship was captured and boarded by a Leeward Republic battlecruiser, and then I got to sort of meet Lin's father—that was weird. And now I get to sit here and be questioned by this guy who looks like he just got out of high school and keeps telling me *I'm* dumb.

Of course, he's a naval intelligence officer—not in *my* Navy, but that doesn't really matter—so he has plenty of experience with stupidity. Whoever originally said that military intelligence is an oxymoron must have been thinking of this kid.

"What do you have to say for yourself, Mr. Mendoza?" he asks, rudely omitting my title. I may no longer be in the Navy, but I'm still the *captain* of a ship.

I shrug, mainly because every time I do, it ticks him off, and that's probably the only fun I'm going to have on this cursed day.

"I'll ask you for the last time: what were you doing in the Fiori system?"

I shrug again, gratified to see his face turn a slightly deeper shade of red. "I was shopping for some drapes. My cabin has a pretty cold aesthetic going on, and I thought I could liven the place up."

He slams both palms down on the table in anger at my flippant response. I don't react; that's the third time he's done that, so it's lost any small shock value it had ninety minutes ago when this little interrogation started.

"I warn you, Mr. Mendoza, until you answer my questions, you're not leaving this room."

Taking a moment to look around the small gray interrogation room, I shrug once again. "I don't know; it's not so bad. My drapes guy could do wonders with that two-way mirror over there; add in a few throw pillows and a duvet, and this space could be downright cozy." Ha! The joke's on him. I have no idea what a duvet is. I just remember my ex-wife, Carla, always talking about us needing a new one.

He doesn't appreciate my amazing sense of humor. But that's alright with me; I decided from the start that his opinion doesn't really matter. Besides, it's fun messing with him, so I lean forward conspiratorially. He can't help it; he leans forward across the table as well.

"Listen," I tell him soberly, "all joking aside, I was actually here smuggling drugs out of the system."

A look of triumph flashes across his face, followed just as quickly by skepticism. He suspects I'm playing an angle. Good.

"And just where would we find these drugs, and what exactly are they?" he asks cautiously.

"In my cargo hold, near the port bulkhead, in a crate marked 'baked beans'." I lean forward more, and he does the same as a natural response. "And I'd rather not say what kind of drugs they are."

He's getting excited, even though he must still suspect I'm pulling his leg. "I don't care if you'd rather say or not," he says with what he probably thinks is a calm, authoritative tone, but his voice cracks a little at the end. "You will tell me now what is in that shipment."

I shrug again and lean forward even more; our faces are less than ten centimeters apart now. "Fine, but I thought you'd want me to exercise a little discretion in a matter like this." I cast a meaningful glance at the two-way mirror behind him.

"Anything you say to me, you can say to the cameras and the other intelligence officers watching," he says.

"OK," I say with an apologetic look, "I was just bringing you your medication; you know, for that little problem you have." I look down in the direction of his lap meaningfully and then back up to savor his reaction.

For a moment, nothing happens; his face is stuck in the grim, authoritative expression he uses when asking me questions. But then, I see understanding dawn, and his eyebrows furrow as his mouth curves down in an angry frown.

I should stop now; I really should. But I'm having way too much fun. "It's nothing to be ashamed of; it happens to the best of us. But I think I got it here not a moment too soon. All the female Marines were talking about your...issue while they escorted me here."

That does it. I thought I made him turn red earlier,

but now he turns a shade of almost purple, and I can see he's about to throw an apoplectic fit. Perfect! I lean back to enjoy the show.

But just as he starts opening his mouth to let forth a no-doubt bloodcurdling but impotent scream, the small room's hatch opens, and an older woman steps in, interrupting the show. I recognize her immediately as the rear admiral who led the boarding party that 'captured' me two hours ago.

"Daniels," the woman says calmly, addressing the stupid intelligence officer, "give us the room."

Admirals have a way of issuing orders without yelling but with no less emphasis, and her simple command is enough to instantly cut off any invectives the guy was about to throw my way. He turns heel without argument and leaves the room, not even giving me a backward glance, though I can tell by the way his shoulders are hunched and his hands balled into fists that he's still raging mad.

"Bye, sweetie!" I yell after him. "I'll see you after work. Don't forget about those pills!"

CHAPTER 2

Interrogated by a Master

The admiral waits for the intelligence officer to leave the room and for the hatch to shut behind him before throwing me a disapproving look that reminds me of my grandmother when she caught me trying to ride one of the dogs on her farm—it was a beagle, and I was nine, but I still thought it might work.

I say nothing but do a pretty good job of keeping a perfectly innocent and beatific expression on my face like I'm a favored student and not the little boy caught pulling the braids of the girl in front of me.

"There is a debate going on, Captain Mendoza," she says calmly—at least *she* remembers to give me my due title, "about just what I should do with you. Our intelligence section would like me to throw you in a very deep and extremely dark hole for the rest of your mortal days while we extract each and every piece of knowledge that may be rattling around in that brain cavity of yours. I suspect that Lieutenant Commander Daniels will be the first to recommend that the particular hole they throw you in be full of Visalian crocodiles."

She pauses, perhaps to give me the opportunity to respond. I choose not to. I want to see where this is going. And I'm still trying not to laugh out loud at the way Daniels left the room a few seconds ago.

To my surprise, she smiles at my silence. "Luckily for you, it just so happens I'm not convinced you would even know enough for it to be worth our trouble."

OK, now I *have* to say something. Because she just called me dumb in a much deeper and more meaningful way than Daniels did. Of course, what I end up saying isn't at all what I would have said had I taken even a moment to consider my words.

"Lady, I know things that would make your head spin." And just like that, it's as if all my SERE training about resisting interrogation never happened.

She raises an eyebrow. "Really? Like what, that big discovery in Gerson that your king is so convinced he's managed to keep under wraps?"

My composure breaks. I just almost died—twice!— to keep the secret of that stellarium deposit, and here she is mentioning it like it's yesterday's news.

"You broke Harris, didn't you?" I demand to know. "I *knew* that guy wouldn't be able to hold up."

"The makeup artist?" she asks incredulously and then sits back in her chair and laughs. She's surprisingly casual and relaxed for a member of the admiralty; maybe they do things differently here in the Leeward Republic. "No," she continues. "I imagine he knows even less than you, but he did go into great detail about what he would change about his interrogator's approach to cosmetics. The look on the poor lieutenant's face when she finally realized he wasn't trying to get under her skin but was actually being serious..." She shakes her head and gives a short laugh.

"Then, Jessica?" I ask, my voice rising an octave because the thought of someone breaking her to the point that she would reveal such valuable information is distressing in the extreme to me.

"Relax, Captain," the admiral says, her tone not rising to meet mine. "Miss Lin hasn't been subjected to the ham-fisted interrogation techniques of our illustrious intelligence directorate. No, she has been with her father this entire time...catching up."

Oh, yeah. Her father. I'm still trying to wrap my head around that one.

As if sensing my thoughts, the admiral gives me a wry smile. "Yes, I imagine you and Lieutenant Commander Lin will have a lot to talk about when you're reunited after all this."

"So, we *will* be reunited?" I ask, unable to keep the hope out of my tone.

She leans forward, and I subconsciously meet her halfway, almost kicking myself when I realize she just used the same tactic on me that I used on poor Daniels moments ago. "Oh, yes, Captain," she says with a thin smile, "you see, I actually have some need of you."

I'm going to ask what she means, but she quickly changes the subject, and I'm starting to realize that when it comes to subtle verbal sparring and keeping your conversation partner off balance, I'm in the presence of a master.

"Tell me, Captain, did you know that the Leeward Republic Naval Academy just added an entire section on your actions at Bellerophon?"

That actually surprises me. "What class, How-Not-to-Captain 101?"

She smirks. "No, actually. Military Ethics 304, one of the advanced classes for our command candidates. And it may not surprise you to hear that there are multiple schools of thought…"

She goes on for a few minutes, and it takes a little while for me to realize that she has cleanly distracted me from the fact that she *knows* about Prometheus' greatest secret, and she supposedly didn't hear about it from Harris or Lin, and she certainly didn't get it from me.

Then how?

"Anyway," she says, "it's an absolutely compelling case of the classic trolley problem; do you divert a trolley to hit one person on a side track to avoid killing five on the main track, or do you…"

I'm still only half listening as my mind races to try and figure things out. Because as near as I can tell, this is all-around *bad* for me and my crew. Not that I really care about good ole King Charles and his stellarium—I'd tell the Leeward Republic or anyone else about it in a heartbeat if I thought it would benefit Lin or me. But even if they *didn't* learn it from us, I know there are many, including one Agent of the King's Cross, Heather Kilgore, who will assume it *was* us who spilled the tea. And that is *not* a woman I want thinking I betrayed her.

But then I realize something else and want to hit my head with the palm of my hand repeatedly, but I refrain lest she think I'm having some sort of episode. She mentioned the *secret* in the Gerson system, but she didn't actually mention the stellarium.

She's fishing.

"…and I'm of the second school of thought, that you made the only choice you could have." She pauses, maybe for air or maybe because she's finally realized I'm not paying attention to her as she dissects the action that ruined my life six-and-a-half months ago.

"You're mistaken," I tell her bluntly. "What I did at Bellerophon was wrong, and there's simply no way to spin it otherwise. I made a bad choice. Period. And 504 civilians died as a result. Tell that to your classroom." The words come easy—strangely so—though I know my tone is bitter. The only other person I've ever said this out loud to was Jessica Lin. But something about the old admiral has put me weirdly at ease. It's the mark of an *excellent* interrogator, and even knowing that she's playing me like a fiddle doesn't change how I react to it.

She considers my response for a second, then shakes her head. "Even your own navy concluded you were innocent of any wrongdoing. Full acquittal."

I frown. "A farce," I say dismissively, having had this particular discussion *many* times with friends and family following the court-martial. "Admiral Oliphant didn't want me dragging his name or his daughter through the mud any more than I already had; he pressured the panel to find in my favor. Politics, pure and simple."

She looks at me, perhaps trying to see if I'm serious, but then surprises me by smiling. The admiral leans forward conspiratorially again, but this time, I stay where I am and don't meet her halfway. "You know," she says, "my father used to say the same two things to every poor boy who

11

picked me up for a date when I was a teenager. First, he'd say, 'Son, there is nothing more powerful than a father's love for his daughter'. Then, he would add, 'Except, that is, for a father's hate for any man not good enough for his daughter'."

She lets that hang there between us for a while as if she expects me to respond. When I don't, she shrugs and stands abruptly. "Well, anyway, I assume you'd like to get back to your crew."

Surprised, I stand slowly, nodding.

She moves to the hatch, and it opens as she nears it, no doubt via some unseen signal to the Marines in the hall. But right before she leaves the room, she turns back to me, her smile gone. "I know you think your father-in-law lobbied for your acquittal. But we had a man in the room, as it were. Terrence Oliphant did, in fact, lobby the panel of judges. But it will surprise you, I imagine, to learn that he lobbied *against* you. Had Oliphant had his way, you would have been convicted and received the death penalty from the King. Something for you to think about."

Before I can respond, she's gone through the hatch, leaving me with my head spinning and with far more questions than answers.

CHAPTER 3

The Damsel in Distress

"**S**he had a giant zit on her forehead, and she used the wrong shade of foundation to try and cover it up. She used Beige Dream, but she should have used Desert Sand." That strange fact enters my earholes courtesy of Harris, the newest member of my crew. It's been three hours since the *Dauntless* stopped my ship and took us all into custody without much in the way of explanation. Now, at least, we're not in interrogation rooms anymore. Instead, a Marine showed me to a small conference room where Harris was already waiting. Since then, for about forty minutes, he's been describing in painful detail the various cosmetic shortcomings of the female lieutenant who tried to interrogate him. The admiral wasn't kidding. I only hope the poor young officer isn't still listening to our conversation, or she might develop a complex.

"Where's Jessica?" I ask aloud for about the fifth time. Harris ignores me—which is fine because I'm asking the microphones no doubt live in this room, not him—and keeps prattling on about his interrogator's split ends or something like that. I think the guy talks when he's nervous. Being woken in the middle of your sleep cycle by a massive battlecruiser capturing and boarding your unarmed ship will do that to a man.

Luckily for both of us, my question is answered promptly this time as the conference room hatch opens and Jessica Lin steps in, her face red and partially hidden by her straight, short black hair, which is hanging forward in a vain effort to hide the puffiness around her stunning green eyes. Despite all that, she's still the most perfect woman I've ever laid eyes on; even the rumpled shipsuit she must have thrown on as we were being boarded can't hide her beauty, nor can the redness of her face hide its perfect proportions or the smoothness of her unblemished skin.

Before I know what I'm doing, I'm out of my seat and standing in front of her, my eyes searching hers for any signs that she's been mistreated, and, finding none, I pull her into a tight hug. I feel her go abruptly rigid, and I quickly realize my mistake and start to unwrap my arms from around her, but suddenly, she grabs me and hugs me back tightly, burying her face in my shoulder.

"Uh, all OK, XO?" I ask.

"All good, Captain," she responds, pushing back from me and blushing as she does so.

We both awkwardly take seats at the conference room table, where Harris has blessedly stopped talking and is now eyeing both of us like we're the characters in some movie he's watching.

"So, what is going on? Why is your father on a Leeward Republic warship?" I ask Jessica.

She looks down at her hands, and I give her the time she needs to formulate a response. But when she finally does speak, it's not very satisfying. "Not here, sir."

I get her point; we have no idea who might definitely be listening in. So, I just nod and turn my attention back to Harris for lack of anything else to talk about.

"Regretting your decision to sign on?" I ask him.

He shrugs. "Owen changed over the years—got meaner and less principled. I wanted to quit his team for a while but couldn't think of a way to do it that didn't end with Tucker bashing in my skull or Jules putting bamboo shoots under my fingernails."

Lovely picture; makes me glad those two thugs are dead.

Harris shrugs again. The constant shrugging really *is* annoying; no wonder Daniels was getting so mad at me. "I mean," he continues, "I wish we weren't on a warship being held against our will and interrogated, but at least we're not doing anything that makes me feel ashamed to be me."

The monumental depth of that statement actually renders me speechless for a few moments as I try to think back to the last time *I* could say I wasn't doing anything that made me feel ashamed to be me. It's been a while, though there have been some brief moments of late.

"Did they mistreat either of you?" Jessica asks, looking back and forth between us like she's scanning for black eyes or tortured souls.

I shake my head. "No. They sent some young intel weenie in to interrogate me, and I'm pretty sure he's reevaluating his life choices now that I've forever ruined his dating life in the Navy." She looks at me funny, but I don't explain further. "But Harris here, he gave his interrogator a complex. She's probably standing in front of a mirror somewhere examining every pore in her face."

Harris grins. "She did have big pores, but she didn't like it when I started counting them. I was just trying to be helpful." This guy. He may seem absent-minded, but I'm becoming increasingly sure he's smarter than he lets on.

At least Jessica seems mollified by our answers, and some of the concern and worry on her face disappears. I'm about to say something to fill the silence when the room's hatch opens again, and the admiral steps in, trailed by a younger woman.

The two sit down without preamble, and the admiral turns to me. "Captain Mendoza, I failed to properly introduce myself earlier. I am Rear Admiral Walters of the Leeward Republic Navy, Fourth Battlecruiser Division, and you are on my flagship, *LRS Dauntless*."

I nod in reply and then motion to Jessica and Harris. As long as the admiral is being civil, I see no reason not to reciprocate. "And as you already know, this is my first mate, Jessica Lin, and our crew member…" I trail off, realizing I actually don't know Harris' first name.

"Harris," he says, not seeming to get the hint. Or maybe he doesn't have a first name, like a music artist. He is weird like that.

Admiral Walter's lip twitches upward in what might be a suppressed smile. But she cuts it off and turns to the young woman in civilian clothes next to her. "This, Captain Mendoza, Commander Lin, and Mr. Harris, is Kayla Carter."

The younger woman nods but says nothing. I study her now. She's short and blond and very attractive—not at the same level as Jessica, but few are. Still, Kayla Carter is quite pretty in a girl-next-door kind of way. She has a small nose surrounded by freckles under dirty blond hair that's pulled back in a messy bun, and her face and arms are tan, the natural kind like she spends a lot of time on the surface of a sunny planet. Her clothing is rough, mostly denim and flannel, and reminds me of the work clothes my grandparents wore around the farm growing up. She turns her head to meet my studying gaze and studies me right back without breaking eye contact, almost in a challenging way.

Admiral Walters continues. "I'm afraid that Miss Carter came to the Republic Navy with some rather disturbing news, and I'd like her to share it with you now."

At that, Kayla Carter breaks eye contact with me and looks around the table. When she speaks, her voice is a soft soprano. "I'm from a small planet called Carter's World. I know what you're thinking, and yes, it's named after one of my ancestors. My father is the current planetary president, but it's an elected position, not hereditary. It's just a matter of tradition that the post often goes to a Carter."

From her homespun clothes and sun-drenched look, I assumed she was an undereducated farmer —like I used to be—but she speaks with clear diction and a steady, confident voice, sounding more like someone educated at one of the universities on a large planet like Prometheus.

"I came here to Leeward Republic space to petition the Navy for aid. Our planet, for the last year, has been under siege by a ruthless group of pirates led by a very nasty man named Poulter. They started small, raiding the occasional freighter coming in and out of the system. Then, six months ago, they escalated things. They destroyed our only system patrol boat and then raided our orbital station, stealing most of the food shipments we had ready for export. They've come back every few weeks since, raiding both the orbital and the planet's surface. They've even brazenly started visiting my father at the presidential mansion and demanding tribute payments. When our small planetary militia tried to stop them on the ground, they strafed our force from one of their ships and killed most of them."

She stops, frowning as if she's reliving that moment. "Now, with outside trade cutoff and our treasury depleted, we're essentially just growing food to feed the pirates and our own populace, but we're short on a lot of vital goods, like medical supplies, that we usually get through trade. If something doesn't happen soon, our people will start dying.

"I barely escaped in our last spaceworthy ship and came to the Leeward Republic," she throws a sour look at Walters, "to petition the Navy for aid, but they have refused to help me."

Walters remains a cool customer, ignoring the woman's piercing gaze. "If it were up to me," the admiral says, "we would take *Dauntless* and deal with these pirates directly. Unfortunately, Carter's World is not a member of the Leeward Republic, nor does it have a mutual defense pact with us. I have explained to Miss Carter that if she were to petition for membership, Republic law would allow me to intervene and help with her situation. But she has made it very clear that she is not empowered to petition on her planet's behalf."

Kayla Carter frowns. "Actually, I've made it clear that even if I could, I wouldn't. We've maintained our independence from the surrounding star nations for seven hundred years, ever since my first ancestor founded the planet. And we will not throw off the shackles of one petty despot for another, no matter how well-intentioned they may appear."

The admiral tactfully ignores the jab at her and her star nation and turns her gaze to me instead. My opinion of Walters keeps rising, and I'm not exactly the biggest fan of admirals in general, so that's saying something. "This is what I was referring to earlier, Captain Mendoza, when I said I had need of you. The Leeward Republic cannot intervene, but perhaps an independent party can."

I return her stare incredulously. "Seriously? What do you expect us to do?" Whether I feel respect for her or not, I can't keep the skepticism out of my tone.

Walters smiles. "Mr. Harris told his interviewer that you're mercenaries, are you not?"

I lean back, sensing a trap. "Well, yeah, but we're

just getting started. And you're talking about a pirate force large enough to hold an entire *planet* hostage. I have..." I look around the table for emphasis, "...two officers, a makeup artist, an unarmed freighter, and two pistols. What do you expect me to do with only that against a force like the one Miss Carter describes? Besides having Harris critique their mohawks and nose rings until they run away in embarrassment, I can't think how we would do any good."

Walters smiles again, and I feel like she's in on a joke that hasn't been shared with me. "Oh, I'm sure you'll figure something out. You seem to be rather adept at that if all the rumors are true."

"And if I say no?" I leave that out there, watching the admiral carefully. Her smile doesn't disappear, but she does raise an eyebrow.

"Well," she says with no hint of malice in her voice, "given that you're foreign nationals in my star nation under false identities and in a ship of dubious origin, I may have to ask Lieutenant Commander Daniels and his intelligence division to dig a little deeper into just what you're doing here. That could take a while. I have a feeling that, in your case, he'll want to be especially thorough. You made such a good impression on him, after all."

She stops, still smiling, but with a look in her eyes that tells me it's my move, and she knows she's backed me into a corner. But I'm in a bad mood, so I open my mouth to argue.

"We'll do it," a firm and resolute voice says. It's not mine, and my mouth now drops open in astonishment as my XO agrees to take the impossible job. I'm going to vocally disagree until I see Jessica shoot me a pleading look, and that shuts me up. She's a sucker for lost causes, apparently, but I'm a sucker for her, so I'll go along with it...for now.

Admiral Walter's smile gets even broader, though Kayla Carter looks from Jessica to me and then to Harris dubiously. And just like that, we're pirate hunters.

CHAPTER 4

A Farmer's Breakfast

I t takes us five jumps and seven days to get to Carter's World from Fiori. For the first two days, we mostly sleep. For me and Jess, it's our first real opportunity to rest since we met Owen Thompson, and we've been running on adrenaline, caffeine, and sheer willpower for more than two full days as we fought for our lives. So now, finally—even if temporarily—out of danger and ignoring how badly I want to talk to her about her father, we crash.

Harris doesn't know how to pilot a ship, but Kayla Carter surprisingly does. Normally, I would never trust someone I don't know to pilot a starship I'm in charge of, but I'm too exhausted to argue. So, she takes on the lion's share of the pilot's duties those first two days while Jessica and I mostly sleep.

On day three, I finally wake up feeling more like

myself than I have in a long time. I'm almost ten days without a drink now, not entirely by choice. And while the withdrawal headaches have been pretty severe, at least my brain is clear. Even though there are still a lot of things I'd love to forget, I'm seriously considering swearing off alcohol altogether. Or maybe I'm just trying to make myself feel better since I'm stuck on this ship for another three days without a drop of alcohol on board.

I leave my cabin and make my way to the galley for breakfast. As I near the room, I can hear someone already there and the sound of what I think is rummaging. Sure enough, I round the corner and enter the door to see Jessica's exquisite rear end in one of *Wanderer's* shipsuits as she's leaning over, going through the refrigerator's bottom shelves. Not a bad way to wake up. I stop to admire it, throwing aside for a moment my personal commitment to stop leering at her. I'm not perfect, after all.

I'm about to reluctantly tear my eyes away when she stands up and looks back at me. To my shock, it's not Jessica; it's Kayla! She sees my surprise and looks me up and down. "Were you just staring at my butt?" she asks sternly.

"I...uh..." My brain shuts down, and the words just aren't coming. Wouldn't you know it, less than three days into my first mercenary job, I've already mortally insulted our client. Finally, I eke out a pathetic "No."

She frowns. "Pity. I've worked hard to make it look this good." My jaw drops open, and she laughs at my expense.

"Come on in," she says playfully, "I'll make you breakfast."

I sit mutely at the table while Kayla bustles around the small galley, and soon, smells that I didn't know could exist on *Wanderer* are making my mouth water. Fifteen minutes later, we're feasting on scrambled eggs and hash browns.

"Where did we get the eggs?" I ask between mouthfuls.

"The *Dauntless* transferred over a bunch of stores right after they fueled up your ship and put that crate in your hold."

Oh yeah, the crate. All Walters would tell me was that it contained some items we would find useful in liberating Carter's World. But it has a location-based lock that won't open for us until we actually reach Kayla's home system. I almost told the admiral to keep it out of suspicion and sheer stubbornness, but Jessica interceded, and cooler heads prevailed.

We eat in silence for a few more minutes, and I get up to grab seconds out of the pan. Kayla finishes eating first and leans back, regarding me with a small frown. "So, you're just starting out as mercenaries?"

I stop the forkful of eggs I was about to bite into and lower it back to the plate. She's trying to keep her tone casual, but from the way her body has tensed up, I know she's truly worried; I would be too in her situation.

"As mercenaries, yes," I admit, "but Jessica and I have plenty of experience fighting pirates in the Promethean Navy."

Kayla raises her eyebrows skeptically. "But didn't you have weapons and warships and even Marines back then?"

She's got me there. But I push the plate away from me and meet her gaze steadily. "We did, but the tactics are still generally the same." It's a lie, but I consider it a harmless one; she needs some sort of assurance right now, even if I legitimately have no idea how we're going to help her and her planet. "How many pirates are there?" I ask, turning the questions back to her.

She frowns. "We're not entirely sure. The most we've seen at any one time was only thirty or so."

"But enough to decimate your planetary militia?"

Kayla nods. "Yes. But you have to understand; besides the fact that the pirates had air support and we didn't, our planetary militia was basically a hundred farmers using weapons older than my great-grandfather. We're a peaceful settlement, and Carter's World has no native large animals, so we don't even hunt for food. And we're a relatively poor farming world, so trading for or buying more and newer weapons has never been a priority."

"Until you needed them," I say.

She sighs loudly. "Until we needed them. You're right. In some ways, we may have brought this upon ourselves by being an easy target. I don't know why we thought a single, barely armed patrol boat would be enough to turn away any trouble coming our way. It was incredibly naïve of us."

It's a startlingly self-aware admission and not one I'm used to hearing from victims. But it's also a self-defeating attitude if allowed to fester, so I decide to cut it off. "Listen, what pirates do, there's no excuse for it, regardless of who the victims are or how the balance of power lies. Besides, I've seen pirate gangs that have dozens of warships and hundreds of well-armed ground troops, so not even a fully-armed destroyer or modern weapons in the hands of a fairly well-experienced militia can hold off every threat. But maybe we can help you out with this one." I have no idea *how* we'll do that, but I'm hoping to at least reassure her.

She smiles now, and it makes her nose crinkle up and accentuates the freckles around it. It's nice and reminds me of my first girlfriend back on Denton III, when I was fourteen. Kayla reaches out a hand and places it on mine. "Thank you, Captain Mendoza. I hope you *can* help us."

Wouldn't you know that very moment, with Kayla Carter's hand on mine and a smile on her face, is when Jessica would show up for breakfast?

"I hope I'm not interrupting," I hear my XO's voice from behind me, and I quickly jerk my hand back, which is not the best move. It makes me look like I was definitely doing something wrong and not just comforting a woman whose entire planet is under attack.

"I…uh…Kayla made eggs. I saved some for you," I say lamely, and Jessica moves wordlessly over to the galley cupboards to grab a plate and start dishing up her breakfast.

Kayla is looking between me and Jessica now, an expression on her face that I can't decipher.

"Umm," I stammer, "I'm going to go to the cockpit and check our course." I get up from the table and beat a hasty exit. Sometimes, I've learned, retreat is the only tactical option a man has.

CHAPTER 5

What Happened on Ordney

L ater, I'm sitting in the cockpit when Jessica joins me, sliding into her co-pilot's seat. She looks as stunning as always, but there's a pensiveness about her that keeps me from opening my mouth. She has something on her mind, and she'll need to decide when it's time to tell me.

We sit like that for five long minutes while I pretend to be busy checking and rechecking and then rechecking our course again. Seriously, there's not much to do on a starship that's beating a straight-line course between jump points in an uninhabited system. So, I'm extremely relieved when Jessica finally decides to start talking and saves me from running a general diagnostic on the ship's systems a *third* time.

"So…about my father…"

I look over at her but say nothing. I try to keep

my expression neutral as well, but I'm sure I'm failing at it. She's about, I hope, to answer some of the burning questions that have dominated my waking thoughts and even a few of my dreams since we were first boarded by the *Dauntless*.

"He's a real piece of work," she says. "I didn't even meet him until I was seventeen. He left my mother while she was pregnant with me."

I manage not to react audibly to that, but my eyebrows shoot up. If Jessica's mother is anything like her, a man would have to be crazy to leave her.

"He's not from Prometheus. He was there for two years as part of a trade delegation from the Leeward Republic. My mother was one of the cultural attaché's assigned to make sure he and the rest of the delegation got whatever they needed while in Promethean space.

"He and Mom grew close, and they even moved in together for his last year on the planet. She got pregnant with me just a few months before his assignment was set to end. I think that having the baby meant Mom naturally assumed he'd either stay with her on Prometheus or ask her to go with him back to the Republic. But…"

She trails off, and I can see pain flash behind her eyes. I want to reach out and comfort her, but I hold back, sensing it would break the spell that has her talking openly right now. This is the first I'm learning much of *anything* about Lin's past—at least, her past before *Persephone* and the little her military file had in it.

She starts talking faster, clearly just trying now to get it all out. "A month before he left, he told Mom she could come with him but that she wouldn't be living with him in the Republic. Turns out he had a whole other *family* there—a wife and kids—and my mom was just the mistress. And he made it abundantly clear she would never be anything more than that. It crushed her, and she told him where he could shove his offer. Then he left. He sent money each year for us, more than enough for us to live very comfortably. Apparently, he came from an extremely wealthy family, and his government work was just part of his training to take over the family business.

"At first, Mom would just send the money back. But as it slowly became clear to her that her government salary wouldn't provide the life she wanted for me, she started keeping the payments. She would spend every credit on me, never on herself. I had the nicest clothes, went to the fanciest private schools, had horse riding and etiquette lessons, and had a full-ride scholarship to the King's University of Prometheus. But it all felt so…claustrophobic, like I was stuck inside her dream for me."

She stops, frowning, and I'm wondering why anyone would *pay* for riding lessons. I can't even remember the first time I rode—I was probably

31

still a toddler—but I'm fairly certain my grandpa just threw me in the saddle, slapped the back of the horse, and told me to hold on tight. I'm sure my father yelled at the old guy after that, but Grandpa never seemed to care what Dad thought, and vice-versa.

"When I decided to reject my scholarship and go to the Naval Academy instead, it nearly killed Mom. At the time, I thought it was her being controlling; now, looking back, I realize that she only wanted what was best for me. Turns out she was right.

"Because just after I accepted my appointment to the Academy, dear old Dad reached out to me for the first time ever." She says that last part bitterly. Still, the way her lip trembles, I can almost feel the hope that a young eighteen-year-old Lin must have had at finally hearing from her absent father.

It's funny how something as simple as a shared genetic code creates such strong expectations of a bond between two people. Even when my own father effectively disowned me after I joined the Navy, I never stopped loving him or longing for his approval. That he died five years later without us ever having a chance to reconcile haunts me to this day. So, I can understand how Lin, even though her father had never shown the slightest interest in her before, had felt so much obvious hope when he'd finally reached out. Unfortunately, I could already see that this story wasn't going to have a happy ending.

"He was on Prometheus for a trade conference, and he asked to see me during his short stop there. I snuck out to meet him because I knew Mom wouldn't approve. I met him at a restaurant near our home, and he was just so...I don't know, perfect, I guess. He said all the right things and even hugged me when he first saw me. I expected him to badmouth Mom, but he never did. He even seemed interested in learning how she was doing. And, unlike her, he was *so* supportive of my decision to join the Navy. I felt like..."

"...like you finally found what you'd been missing?" I finish for her when it's clear she's struggling for the words. Because that's the feeling I always longed for with my own father but never found.

She nods, and I can see she's crying now. Again, I long to reach out and comfort her, but I don't want to overstep like I did in the *Dauntless's* conference room. After all Lin's been through, and despite her briefly hugging me back on *Dauntless*, I know that she has to be the one to initiate any physical contact with a man, and I'm doing my best to respect that, though every part of me often yearns to take her in my arms.

Jessica takes a deep breath and lets it out slowly through pursed lips like she's struggling for oxygen. Then she turns and looks at me. "It was all a lie," she says so softly I can barely hear her. "He played me. We'd get together every six months or so, usually on Prometheus between deployments. He always seemed really interested in my naval service, but I didn't tell him anything classified or secret, and he didn't press.

"Then, one day, I got a note from him that he was coming to the Federation again and *really* needed to talk to me about something. He sent the note to Prometheus, and I got it a few days later, forwarded to me on *HMS Ordney* in the Kipling system, where I was deployed. In my return message, I told him that we would have to wait a couple of months until my next leave, but he wrote back so insistent. He said that what he needed to talk to me about couldn't wait. We went back and forth a few times until finally I gave him a day and time to meet me in the Hothan system, our next patrol stop. I thought it wouldn't do any harm."

Tears are flowing down her face now, and I'm practically holding my breath, unable to believe that I finally might be hearing about what happened on *Ordney* that ruined Jessica's career.

"He didn't show..." she says in a gasping sob. "He —"

An alarm sounds in the cockpit, causing us both to jump in surprise. My first thought is that *Dauntless* followed us from Fiori and is going to repeat its forced docking maneuver again—maybe that intel weenie, Daniels, finally convinced Admiral Walters that I'm too dangerous to roam free, or maybe she decided it was time to forcefully extract the information about Gerson from me—but a quick check of the cockpit displays dispels that notion.

The real reason for the alarm, however, is perhaps more concerning, even if it comes in a deceptively polite package.

"Congratulations!" I read out loud from the display. "Your StarHauler model TK421 has reached a thousand hours of jump time. It's time for your first service appointment. To ensure your safety and the proper break-in of your advanced Gorendi 6000 jump drive, you only have one more jump before the drive will auto shut down until a licensed StarHauler service technician has certified that its one-thousand-hour maintenance is complete. Please proceed directly to the nearest system with a licensed StarHauler service center. And have a great day!"

Jess and I look at each other. And whether it's the fact that we just went from the grim to the absurd in no time flat or because we both just really need something to distract us, we burst out laughing together.

CHAPTER 6

Fixing Our Dumb Ship

W e're not laughing for long. Because now we have a really big problem. The service catalog on Wanderer apparently never assumed anyone would operate the ship this far out in the Fringe because it doesn't list a single licensed StarHauler service center within five jumps of our current location. And we only have one jump until the drive shuts down.

"Just override it!" Lin says in exasperation. Whenever she has a problem to solve, she transforms into Confident Lin, and right now, Confident Lin is taking all of the emotional frustration she's been feeling from reuniting with her father and instead directing it toward this problem. Unfortunately, that means she's taking at least some of it out on me.

"I thought of that," I explain, my own exasperation

mirroring hers. "But it's a civilian ship, not a warship. And apparently, StarHauler's desire to keep its customers safe *and* bilk them out of money with required service overrode any concern the company had for its customers completing vital missions to rescue planets and damsels in distress from mean pirates."

Jessica grunts and reaches out to slap the console in front of her in frustration. It's the most violent reaction I've ever seen out of her, but I pretend not to notice. Instead, I peer more closely over her shoulder at the menu of options on that same abused console. We're in *Wanderer's* small engineering compartment, and so far, nothing we've tried has allowed us to bypass the ship's dogged commitment to shut down our jump drive after our next jump.

"What if we just yanked out all the fuses and forced the computer to reset?" Lin asks next as I try to read some incredibly small print about power conduits and fusion reactor maintenance. Unfortunately, every single paragraph I've read thus far ends with the same infuriating statement: 'Please do not attempt to service [insert random system here] on your own. Contact a licensed StarHauler service center'. Terrific.

"It won't work," I tell her. "Or it might, but it could also scramble the computer so badly that we won't even get that one jump. What's the largest inhabited system we could get to in a single jump?"

She consults her implant for a moment. "Jeffrey's Landing. It's got two stations, including a shipyard. Very promising. But it's in the Jutzen Protectorate."

I frown. Even in Prometheus, we've heard about the Jutzen Protectorate, and I'm not that keen on trusting my ship and my crew in a system controlled by jingoistic neo-Nazis. "Next," I tell her.

"Literally, the only other option big enough to have even basic repair facilities is Boral. But if we can't find what we're looking for there, we're completely out of luck. Are you sure you don't want to try the Nazis?"

"Oh yeah. One hundred percent sure."

She nods, which I take to be agreement. "OK. Boral it is, then. I'll lay in the course." She leaves to head back forward to the cockpit.

I spend a few more minutes going through more nonsensical menus on the engineering console, doing anything right now to distract myself from the fact that if we can't magically find a licensed StarHauler technician in Boral—and I've never even heard of Boral—then our little mission, and even our entire future as mercenaries or anything else, is over before it even had a chance to get started.

As I continue my frustrated scrolling, I hear someone enter the small room. "Forget something?" I ask, expecting Jessica.

"What are you doing down here? Is the ship OK?"

I look up in surprise to see Kayla. She looks like someone just woke her from a nap. Her blond hair is mussed, and she's wearing a soft-looking t-shirt, a pair of cutoff shorts, and no shoes. She looks oddly terrific.

"Uh, sorry," I say, flustered, "did we wake you?"

She nods but smiles to show there are no hard feelings. "What are you doing down here? Is everything OK with the ship?" she repeats her earlier question.

"Oh, uh," I look from her back down to the console and then back at her. "Sure. All good. We just have to make an unscheduled stop."

Kayla frowns and crosses her arms, pulling herself up to her full 162-centimeter height. It shouldn't be intimidating, but I have the sudden mental image of my grandma scolding me for throwing newly laid eggs at a target I drew on the side of the barn when I was eleven. "You're lying," she says simply. "What's going on, Brad?"

I'm honestly not sure when she and I got to a first-name basis, but I don't give it much thought. "Well…we kind of have a problem with the star drive."

Kayla says nothing but walks over to peer into the inner workings of the main engine. She fixates on a power conduit and follows it across the small room until it terminates in a large metal box. "Hmm, is that a Gorendi 6000?"

The question takes me aback. "Yeah, it is. How did *you* know that?" I don't mean to make it sound the way it does, but the question leaves my lips before I can stop it.

She raises an eyebrow. "What, because I'm a woman? Or because I'm a hick from a dead-end farming world where we only know about sheep, cattle, and kissing our cousins?"

"Uhhh." There's no answer I can give here that won't get me in trouble.

Then she surprises me by smirking. "Relax, flyboy, I'm just messing with you. I studied starship engineering at the University of New Rottendam. We do have starships in Carter's World—or we did before the pirates showed up. Someone had to keep them running."

She walks over to me, bumping me aside with one hip as she peers at the console readout. She starts manipulating the display and skimming through the text, grunting, nodding, and frowning at various parts. Then she looks back up at me with another smirk. "Got the old 'pay us tons of money to service the drive, or we'll shut you down' message, huh?"

I nod dumbly.

"And you were going to fly to the next system over

and try and find a mechanic who could service it?"

I nod again.

She shakes her head and laughs. "And here I thought you were ex-navy and knew something about ships."

I shrug. "I know how to fly them and shoot things. We had engineers for all the other stuff."

She laughs again, and it's a good sound, especially after the gloominess that Jessica and I shared earlier and the sense of despair since the service message. "Boy, there's a sucker born every minute." She pecks at the console for another few moments, and I see her pull up some kind of root menu that I was never able to find and probably still couldn't even after watching her. Then, about a minute or so later, she looks back up with a wry smile. "And, done. No more drive shutdown. You can thank me by walking me back to my quarters, flyboy." I guess I have a new nickname now. I'm not sure how I feel about that.

Do you ever get the sense that you're completely out of your depth, like there's some big joke in the universe that everyone else is in on but you? That's how I feel every second with Kayla Carter. Sure, she's attractive, but I'm in love with Jessica, so I don't think it's that. It's more the way Kayla talks and teases me like I'm still the young farm boy with dreams of being a mercenary like my hero, Billy Firebrand.

So, I don't say anything but follow her dumbly out of the engineering space and the short distance down the corridor to the door to her quarters. And I have to admit, I'm watching her tan, toned legs a bit as she walks in front of me.

She turns right at the hatch to her quarters and smiles at me. "Thanks, Brad. See you at dinner? I'm cooking chicken cacciatore."

I nod, not trusting my voice right now, and she smirks again and reaches up to cup my chin in one hand like she's examining a small child with dirt on his face. Then she releases me and opens the hatch to her room, enters, and shuts it behind her without a backward glance.

I shake myself out of my stupor and make my way to the cockpit, all sorts of confusing emotions clashing in me, to tell Jessica she can return us to our original course.

CHAPTER 7

Eavesdropping

T he final two days of our journey pass uneventfully, even in boring fashion. I try a few times to get Jess to talk about her father again, but she changes the subject each time. Whatever moment we shared in the cockpit doesn't repeat. Instead, we spend a few hours here and there talking about old Navy missions or Promethean officers we both knew, but we run out of common friends quickly and often lapse into silence, both doing our best to pretend there isn't a massive elephant in the room.

Kayla, on the other hand, is a whirlwind of nervous energy the closer we get to her home system. She seems to deal with her nerves by cooking, pacing the ship's single long corridor, and generally trying to engage just about anyone she can in conversation.

Harris learns the hard way that he can't hold his own with her. A pretty shy guy normally, I can see that interacting with Kayla breaks his introvert brain, and he spends most of the last two days hiding in his quarters. And Jessica, who is reserved at the best of times, and this isn't one of those times for her, soon starts to avoid Kayla like a plague.

Which leaves me.

At first, I tell myself I should also be annoyed by the bubbly young woman. But soon, I find I can't even fake not enjoying it because Kayla is just so... different. We talk about so many things as she literally follows me around the ship that I feel like I know her almost as well as I ever knew anyone aside from Carla.

We spend a lot of time, in particular, talking about farming. And for a guy who literally joined the Navy so I *didn't* have to take over the farm from my grandpa or be an accountant like my dad, I find it oddly comforting to talk about something from my past life. Maybe it's because my past life is irretrievably over. I'm still legally dead, even if it seems everyone I come across knows who I really am.

As we go, I can feel something growing inside me. It's strange because my unrequited feelings for Jessica haven't diminished in the least, and I can't imagine life without her, even after less than three weeks together.

Still, with Kayla, everything is just so natural and easy. Even though I can see her worrying about her family and what we'll find when we arrive at Carter's World, she still seems so upbeat. She also flirts with me, a *lot*. And while I know it shouldn't, that makes me like being around her even more. It's nice sometimes to feel wanted.

So now I somehow have feelings for two women at once, and while I still, in moments of self-reflection, know that my feelings for Jessica are the much stronger of the two, I can't ignore what I'm starting to feel for Kayla. Which makes me, honestly, feel like a horrible human being. Am I really so desperate to be loved that I'll let my affections shift so quickly? Or that I'll go for another woman simply because she's available and willing?

It all comes to a head on our last night before we arrive in Kayla's home system. Jessica and I have been alternating sleep schedules again, so one of us is always awake in case something goes wrong in the cockpit, even when Kayla is flying the ship. It's about eight in the evening, and my next shift doesn't start for another four hours, but I awake in my bunk and can't fall back asleep. Maybe it's pre-mission jitters, or maybe it's just that I'm getting older and can't sleep on command at strange hours anymore. Either way, I'm awake, and I'm hungry.

My plan is to grab a snack, take it back to my quarters, and try again to sleep, so I don't dress or even put shoes on. I walk out into the corridor in stocking feet and make my way toward the galley.

Now, *Wanderer*, for all of her charm, is not a luxurious ship by any stretch of the imagination. And nowhere is that more apparent than her deck. The floor of the corridor is basically a two-centimeter-thick metal grate that covers conduits full of power cables and environmental systems. That means that you can usually hear someone walking from almost anywhere on the small ship. But in my socks alone, I make almost no sound as I approach the galley, making it quiet enough for me to hear the voices before they can hear me coming.

I'm surprised to hear that Jessica and Kayla are in the galley together. Apparently, Jess didn't manage to dodge the talkative young farm girl slash engineer, or maybe she just wanted some of Kayla's cooking badly enough to put up with her chatter.

No matter how it happened, it's happening, and I subconsciously slow and creep up to the door, listening in on their conversation.

"So, are you excited to see your family?" my XO asks our passenger.

"I am, well, mostly. It's just my dad, really. Mom died a few years back, and my brother died in an accident before I was born. So, I'm all he has, and I'm just not sure he can manage without me there."

"He obviously did fine while you were away at school."

I hear Kayla laugh at Jessica's observation. "Well, he didn't starve, if that's what you mean. But I also don't think he wore a matching outfit the whole two years I was gone. Some of his press conferences were...interesting. He looked more like a beggar than a president. But everyone is so in awe of the Carter family name that I don't think even his own staff were willing to tell him just how ridiculous he looked." She laughs again, and I can tell the memory is a good one for her.

"Well, I'm sure he'll be glad to have you home then." Jess's response is a little less enthusiastic, and I know she's probably thinking of her own father and whatever passed between them to destroy her relationship with the man.

Kayla doesn't seem to notice Jessica's sudden shift in mood. "It'll be so good to see him." Then, she abruptly changes the subject. "So...Brad?"

"What about him?" Lin's tone is suddenly guarded.

"Well, I'm not sure how to ask this, but...are you and he...?" The unfinished question hangs in the room between them, and I can almost feel the tension even without seeing the expression on either woman's face.

Jessica is slow to answer, and when she does, it's in the crisp, professional tone she seems to use whenever an overly personal matter comes up and she's trying to deflect. "No. We're not. It wouldn't be appropriate, given he's my commanding officer. And besides, he and I...well, I don't know. But no, we're not together."

The words spear me through the heart like a hot knife, and my knees go weak. I had thought that the whole 'no fraternizing between officers' had ended when we both literally *died* and left the Navy. But apparently, Jessica doesn't think that way. And the way she's so quickly dismissed Kayla's comment, it feels like she just shut the door forever on any possibility of us being more than what we are now.

Honestly, I've known since before the Rishi Paradise that Jessica was never likely to love me back the way I love her. But hearing her actually say the words is painful in the extreme, and I'm trying hard not to gasp for breath in the corridor and betray to both of the women that I've been listening in.

"Oh, that's..." Kayla starts but seems unsure of how to respond to Jessica's statement. Instead, she pushes forward awkwardly. "So, you wouldn't mind if I... Well, I like him. And I think he may like me, too. I just didn't want to start anything if you and he were...you know."

"Well, we're not," I hear Jess say with a painful, almost angry finality. Then I hear her stand from the galley table and start walking across the room.

I beat a hasty retreat and duck back into my cabin hatch an instant before she enters the corridor where I was hiding.

Inside my room, I stand with my back to the hatch, fighting to control my breathing and my emotions. Because I feel like my whole world, the little that I've been able to reconstruct since the disaster at Bellerophon has now crashed down around me... again.

CHAPTER 8

Pirates!

J essica and I are both quiet, engrossed in our own thoughts, when Wanderer exits jump space in Carter's System. It actually has another name on the star charts, but Kayla assures us everyone just calls the system the same basic name as the planet.

She's in the cockpit with us, too, and is abnormally silent herself. Harris is even here, though he looks lost. I guess there wasn't much time spent in ship cockpits for a makeup and disguise expert who somehow fell in with mercenaries. Though he's also mentioned a few times that Owen used him as a technology expert; I may need to unpack that with him.

"Scanning," Jess says crisply as *Wanderer* reenters normal space.

"Bringing the main drive back online," I reply.

We continue back and forth like that, falling into old habits and patterns that provide a sense of comfort to me. I'm still reeling from what I heard Jessica tell Kayla, and I'm wishing for all the universe that I had a bottle of scotch on board. But in the absence of my normal solace, I'm finding consolation in the mundane.

"Ship detected!" Jessica exclaims, breaking me from my concentration on spinning up our main engine. "Unknown class, bearing one oh four mark two relative."

I check the sensor picture and see the same thing she does. The ship in question appears to be burning hard on a vector from the outer system like it was waiting just behind the jump point for anyone exiting it.

We've been in Carter's System for all of thirty seconds, and the pirates have already found us.

Of course, we knew this could happen. There are only so many jump points into and out of any given system, and the number is pretty random, though the more populated systems seem to have more simply by virtue of being more heavily explored. But Carter's System only has two known jump points, which has made it very easy for the pirates to blockade the entire place.

In our favor, however, is the fact that through some quirk of celestial mechanics that no scientist has ever been able to adequately explain, a ship exiting jump space maintains the same velocity as when it entered the jump. And we purposefully set ourselves up to come in hot.

"Time to intercept?" I ask my XO, even though my own console would just as easily give me the answer. Division of duties is as important on our freighter as it was on the bridge of any warship we've ever crewed. It keeps us all focused on the right things and avoids duplication of effort that often can lead to disaster when other important items go unnoticed.

"If we go full burn, eight hours. We've got a velocity advantage on them, but they can outdo our acceleration by about seventeen percent, assuming what we're seeing now is their max."

"Great. Options people?"

I'm really asking just Jessica, but having learned how to conn a starship on the bridge of many a warship, I'm used to having a larger command crew. Luckily for me, Kayla takes my question literally.

"Big Ben," she says, causing both Jess and I to turn in our seats and regard her in confusion. "It's that gas giant over there," she continues, pointing through the forward viewport at a star that's significantly brighter than all but the system's own primary; it's also about as far away as you can get from the planet of Carter's World, but that's beside the point.

"When I was learning to pilot an in-system shuttle," Kayla continues, "one of the old salts told me stories of smugglers who used to come through back when we actually had a small system patrol fleet. Supposedly, they used to hide in Big Ben's upper atmosphere because the ionization wreaked havoc on the patrol ship sensors, and the dense gases hid them from visual scans as well."

I look over at my XO. Jessica consults her implant and nods. "At full burn, we can get there in a little over six hours. It's cutting it close, but unless they have long-range ship killer missiles on that little boat, we should be able to do what Miss Carter's suggesting before they can get within weapons or boarding range." She turns and regards Kayla again. "That is, of course, assuming you're right."

I can almost hear Kayla bristle behind me, and I do hear the deep breath she takes in as she prepares to argue, so I jump in before she can. "Let's do it. XO, set a course. Main drive is coming online now, and we'll go full burn. Kayla, you're the closest thing we have to an engineer, so I want you back with the engines in case something goes wrong." That'll keep her and Jessica separate for now. "Harris," I look back at him, "find a fire extinguisher or something in case we take damage."

Harris immediately unbuckles from his seat and heads aft to do as instructed. Kayla lingers for a moment, and I'm afraid she's going to object to being relegated to the engineering space. But after only a second or two, she unbuckles as well and follows after Harris, leaving me and Jessica alone.

"Any other options?" I ask now that Kayla is out of earshot.

Lin shakes her head. "No. We knew they'd probably be waiting for us, but I honestly didn't think they'd risk being that *close* to the jump point. It's reckless. What if we'd drifted that direction on exit? Either way, if they'd been just a little further out, we might have made the planet or even the other jump point before they could catch us, but now…" she shrugs. "Now we'll just have to hope Miss Carter knows what she's talking about."

I nod grimly. "Well, let's game out some contingency plans in case it doesn't work." But after thirty minutes of that, we both surrender and admit that we only have one option. Now, all we have to do is wait five and a half more hours to see if that option means we get to live today.

CHAPTER 9

Another Stupid Plan

F ive and a half hours gives us plenty of time to examine the pirate ship chasing us, even with the Wanderer's commercial-grade scanning suite. What we see isn't encouraging. According to Kayla, the citizens of Carter's World have seen two different pirate ships at various times. A big one and this smaller one that's chasing us now.

But even though it's the smaller of the two, the scanner readings on the ship chasing us are enough to tell us that we've likely bitten off more than we can chew.

"Really, they have cold reaction thrusters?" I ask incredulously. What I would have given to have had those on *Persephone*, and she was a warship... well, sort of.

"And some pretty serious retro boosters," Jessica

says solemnly. "Not to mention, those really look like missile tubes to me." She points at a few dark circles on the visual scan image.

"Agreed. This isn't the rough-and-tumble variety of pirates I was hoping to find, with ships cobbled together from spare parts. That boat looks like it probably started life as part of some system's patrol fleet. Maybe the pirates stole it somehow or just bought it surplus from a mothball fleet, but if that's the case, they've upgraded a few things. Whoever these guys are, they're well-financed."

Jessica is silent after that, and I can see she's working through some things on her implant. I busy myself rechecking a few indications on the sensor reading, giving her the time she needs to think. I've learned that Jessica Lin's brain, when engaged in solving a problem, is a truly beautiful and dangerous thing. I always considered myself a good tactician before I became a drunken mass murderer, but I've caught glimpses enough of my XO's brilliance that I have to admit she's better than I ever was. The problem is in helping her believe in herself enough to put that genius to work.

For the thousandth time, I find myself mentally cursing Commander Yancy Jessup, Lin's former commanding officer, and Petty Officer Nedrin Jacobs, the king's rapist nephew, for all they did to Jessica on *Persephone*. Likewise, I find myself cursing her father, who obviously had something to do with whatever happened before that on the destroyer *Ordney* that ruined her career and robbed her of whatever self-confidence she may have previously had.

I prod her gently. "What's going on in that head of yours, XO?"

We're nearly to the gas giant now, and in about twenty minutes will enter its upper atmosphere. We can't see it through the forward viewport, though, as we're turned over and facing away from Big Ben, letting our main drive burn hot to decelerate us enough from our mad dash so that we won't either skip off the atmosphere or break up upon entry.

"I was just thinking," she replies, her voice professional and firm like it was when she came up with the plan to take out that Koratan scimitar-class destroyer we encountered in the Gerson system. "Even if our ruse works, that pirate can almost certainly wait us out. All he has to do is position himself between us and Carter's World to intercept us. And if he calls in backup, a second ship could do the same with the jump point. We'd be stuck with no way out other than a run to the outer system, and he'll catch us with his better acceleration in any extended chase."

I nod. I've been thinking much the same thing but decided that was a problem for Future Brad. Present Brad is just trying to survive the next twenty minutes. But, as usual, Jessica is thinking four steps ahead. "So, what do we do about it?" I ask.

"What if we could make him think we didn't survive entry to the gas giant's atmosphere?"

It's a good thought but not concrete enough to take action on yet. "Go on," I tell her.

"I think if we jettisoned a few things out the airlock, we could make it look like debris from damage. Then we could flare the drive and simulate an explosion."

Whoa. The first part, I'm totally with her; but the second? It's pretty stupid. But, as usual, stupid may be all we have to work with. Fitting, considering our captain.

"Let me get this straight," I say slowly. "You want to purposefully light the atmosphere around us on fire?"

She grimaces but nods resolutely, and despite the sheer audacious idiocy of the plan, seeing Confident Lin make an appearance gives me a little thrill.

"OK, OK," I say. "But we'll need perfect timing, or we'll go boom along with the atmosphere around us."

"On it, sir. You get us to Big Ben in one piece, and I can make that pirate ship think we didn't survive entry."

CHAPTER 10

Lighting Stuff on Fire

"Ten seconds, Commander Lin!" I call out, subconsciously reverting back to her old Navy title. "You ready?"

"Ready, sir!" she responds from the co-pilot's seat.

"Harris, you ready?" I ask through the intercom.

"We're ready," Kayla answers for the man. Seriously, if I don't find Harris something constructive to do soon, I'm not going to be able to justify even having him on the ship breathing our air and eating our food. It's surprising how *seldom* we find ourselves in need of a good makeup artist.

As the seconds count down, I quickly imagine what Billy Firebrand, my favorite fictional mercenary, would say in this situation. Probably something really cool and pithy right as we hit the gas giant's atmo. I need to come up with something just as good.

"Let's get some!" I call out as the timer hits zero. I hear a startled grunt from Jessica next to me, but she doesn't thankfully waste any time trying to figure out what I mean—which is good because even *I* have no idea what I was trying to say there—and instead cries out, "Harris, Kayla, now!" and then hits a button on her console to run a preprogrammed routine.

Three things happen in quick succession. First, our main drive cuts out. We've already turned back over to hit the atmosphere nose-first, so to the pirate behind us, it will look like a drive failure —we hope. Second, Harris—or probably Kayla— overrides the airlock controls and slams open the outer hatch, and the near vacuum still around *Wanderer* forcibly sucks out the air that was in the airlock, and with it, the various odds and ends we piled in there. Unfortunately, we didn't exactly have many things on the ship to start with, so the gas giant just got most of our dishes, some spare hull plating kept in the cargo hold for repairs, some canned foodstuffs, and most of our collective wardrobes. I say a silent prayer of thanks and farewell to the red dress Jessica wore at the Rishi Paradise. I'm going to miss that dress most of all. But hopefully, our improvised 'debris' is enough to help sell this.

Third and final, our drive roars back to life just as the airlock closes again. It's only on for a split second, but it's on at full burn, and burn it does. Because now we're just deep enough in the atmosphere that the heat and fire from our drive going at max thrust, even for a moment, is enough to ignite every particle of air within five hundred meters of our little ship.

I cringe as I imagine the fire engulfing us and burning *Wanderer* and then each of us to so much gooey slag and ash. Luckily, our forward momentum is enough to mostly outrun the maelstrom, and I keep us on a fixed course deeper into the atmosphere. Then, hopeful that we're deep enough to be out of sight and sensor range, I hit the retro thrusters and slow our mad descent into Big Ben's gassy depths.

We're alive, though maybe barely. Now, we just have to hope that it actually worked.

CHAPTER 11

A Lot of Gas

I n the movies, Wanderer would be able to hover in place, just at the right depth to prevent detection, while the heroes inside pat themselves on the back and have a good meal.

This isn't the movies, and sad to say, most starships aren't all that good at hovering, especially in the gravitational well of a gas giant with its wind speeds measured in the hundreds of kilometers per hour.

So, the only way we can maintain our little ship at the correct depth—just deep enough to hopefully be invisible to the pirates above but shallow enough to, at some point, be able to reach escape velocity and break the grip of the massive planet's gravity—is to fly almost recklessly fast in what is essentially a very low orbit.

With the high winds and the sudden increases and

drops in atmospheric pressure that threaten to send us up and down by several hundred meters at a time, that means I'm in a constant state of white-knuckle panic at the wheel. It really sucks.

After four hours of it, my hands have cramped so hard that they're practically locked onto the control yoke, and the sweat is pouring down my face in veritable rivers. At that point, Jessica finally convinces me to let her take the helm.

It's not that I don't trust her, but when you're the captain of a ship—any ship—you feel a responsibility to do the really hard stuff yourself, especially when so much is on the line. Strange, again, that I find myself falling back into those old patterns of command I thought I lost after Bellerophon.

I stumble out of the cockpit and head down the corridor to the galley. As tired as I am and as badly as I just want to fall into my bunk until I have to take over from Jessica in a few hours, I know my body needs nourishment as much as it needs sleep. My plan is to grab a few ration packs and stuff them down on my way back to my quarters, but I enter the galley to find Kayla there with a steaming plate of something that smells amazing.

I sit down at the table without a word, my body still shaking from the stress, and she sets the plate in front of me. I start eating ravenously, and I'm sure it's about the least attractive thing in the world, but she moves around the table and slides onto the bench next to me, sitting close. As I'm shoving food into my mouth, she starts to lightly caress my back with her fingertips.

It's always been an internal debate for me whether or not women understand what they're doing to men when they tickle or lightly scratch our backs. Carla used to do it absent-mindedly while we watched movies together on the couch during my rare times home from deployment, and it drove me crazy in a good way every time.

Now, with Kayla doing it to me here, it starts to relax my aching muscles ever so slightly, and I'm suddenly very aware of her hip touching mine as she sits so close to me. My brain is foggy, as if I've just drunk half a bottle of whiskey, and I'm so tired and stressed that I'm amazed I have any capacity left for rational thought. But the small part of my brain that is still capable of anything is screaming at me to think and not act.

However, it's only a small part, while the rest of me is looking for a release—any release—from the stress of the past few hours. Couple that with the aching pain I still feel at hearing Jessica last night in the galley telling Kayla there would never be anything between us, and I'm in a pretty vulnerable and raw state, I suppose.

I don't know who initiates it, but suddenly, Kayla and I are kissing. It's not for long, and I'm the one to break it off, but it ends with her snuggling into my side contentedly while I try to figure out what just happened and regain interest in the meal in front of me.

There's a voice in the back of my head now, whispering all sorts of things to me. If I listen to that voice, the next thing that will happen is pretty obvious. But there's another voice in my head arguing against that. It's my mother's, and I can hear her almost as if she were in the room, telling me what she told me on my seventeenth birthday when my girlfriend at the time and I were starting to get serious: 'Son, you can always wait, and if it's meant to be, it will still be there when you're done waiting. But if you act too soon, you can never take that back.'

And the truth is, I still love Jessica. Even after hearing what she said last night, I'm not willing to give up on her yet. I honestly don't know if I ever will be. Part of me wonders if that's because she *is* so unattainable, and I see some sort of challenge in that. But my mind also keeps going back to the night we laughed and told stories in the cockpit while transporting Owen Thompson and his crew into the Fiori system. Even in my conversations of late with Kayla, I've rarely felt so in sync with another person as I did that evening with Jessica. On top of that, even just in the three weeks since I met her on *Persephone*, we've been through an incredible amount together. Am I willing to throw that all away just for the chance of sleeping with a girl I just met?

No. I'm not.

So, with a little regret, I gently disengage myself from Kayla, carry my plate to the sink, and then mumble something about how tired I am before I leave the galley and go collapse in my bunk...alone.

CHAPTER 12

Bombs

Three hours later, my alarm jolts me awake, and I make my way out of my quarters and back into the galley. I'm equal parts disappointed and relieved that Kayla isn't there waiting for me, but she or perhaps Harris has recently started a new batch of coffee, so I help myself to two full cups to shake off the sleep. Then, I go up to the cockpit to check on Lin.

Jessica doesn't even acknowledge me when I sit down in the chair next to her. Her red-rimmed eyes are locked on the console in front of her where the instrument readings give the only indication of where we are; the swirling gases of Big Ben's atmosphere block any meaningful view out the forward viewscreen. Lin's hands, similar to mine before, are gripping her control yoke so tightly that her knuckles have turned stark white, and I can see tremors in her arms from the fatigue and stress of constantly having to adjust the ship's course to keep us at the proper altitude.

"Do you think they're gone yet?" I ask softly, mostly as a way to make sure she knows I'm even there.

"No way to know unless we want to risk popping up where we can see. But then they'll see us if they haven't left yet." Her voice is shaky, and there's a desperate edge to it that I can relate to.

I grunt in agreement. Reluctantly, I pull up the proper view on my console and then put my hands around the control yoke. With an audible gasp of relief, Jessica relinquishes control to me and slumps back in her seat, panting from the last four hours of exertion.

Ten minutes later, just as I'm starting to feel the pain from muscles already clenched too tightly in my shoulders, back, and arms, she finally seems to have recovered enough of her wits and motor functions to leave. She gets up and, using the backs of the seats for support, starts to make her way to the cockpit hatch.

"Jess," I stop her, "what happened on *Ordney* with your father?"

I'm horrified the moment the words leave my lips. I don't know why I've chosen this exact moment to ask it, but the words are out now, and there's no taking them back.

"I..." she trails off, and I wisely keep my mouth shut and don't prod her further. But she also doesn't leave the cockpit yet. I can't see her; I can't afford to take my eyes off my console readout long enough to even glance back at her, but I can almost feel her staring out the forward viewscreen at the roiling gases beyond. "I'm sorry, Brad," she says, but there's none of the expected anger or annoyance in her tone; she just sounds tired. "I might be able to tell you the rest of the story one day, but I'm just not ready to tell *anyone* about it quite yet. I hope that's OK?"

"Yeah, of course, Jess." Why is she asking me if that's OK? Seriously, she should be yelling at me for asking such a deeply personal question while we're both exhausted and chasing pirates.

But instead, I feel her hand land on my shoulder and squeeze it lightly. "Thanks," she says, and then she's gone.

An hour later, I hear someone come back into the cockpit, but I can't turn to see. Hands land on my shoulders and start massaging them.

"When do you think we'll be able to leave the atmosphere?" Kayla asks behind me.

I take a deep breath, letting it out, which she probably interprets as my exhaustion or a sign that I'm enjoying the shoulder rub. Truth be told, I definitely am. I would just enjoy it more if it was Jessica giving it. But as the knots work out of my shoulders, I'm very grateful, and in my frantically overwrought state, I start to have some more very warm thoughts about my cute passenger.

"I don't know," I answer honestly. "Maybe we can try in another few hours and see if they've left, but we'll only get—"

I'm cut off when *Wanderer* jolts to one side as a bomb goes off.

CHAPTER 13

We Need a New Plan

T he explosion rocks the ship, almost sending our little freighter off course completely before I'm able to correct and prevent a dive deeper into the atmosphere. My first thought is that something has happened to the engines, and I have a flashback to the ion drive failing on Persephone as we made the mad run from the Koratan destroyer in Gerson. But this explosion feels different to me, and I soon ascertain why.

By that time, a second and then a third explosion have rocked the ship, and Kayla is no longer rubbing my shoulders. Instead, I hear her sit in the seat behind me and strap herself in. To her credit, she otherwise makes no sound and doesn't panic.

Lin rushes back into the cockpit and wordlessly takes her seat next to me. By how quickly she arrived, she must have been lying awake or even in the galley eating.

"Proximity mines," I say through gritted teeth.

Jessica swears, the first time I've actually heard her use that kind of language, and Kayla yelps in surprise as a fourth and then a fifth explosion hit *Wanderer* like the fists of an angry deity.

"They know we're alive then," Jessica says, and I nod rigidly.

"It's a pretty good bet."

"What are we going to do?" Kayla asks from behind us, her voice cracking from stress.

"We have to go deeper," Jessica answers for me. "They've obviously been able to see us, at least to some degree, and they've gotten ahead of us and mined our orbital path."

"Why don't we just shift our orbit laterally?" I hear Harris ask, though I'm unsure when he actually arrived in the cockpit.

"Can't," Jessica answers again. "Or rather, we can, but there's no guarantee they won't be able to see us again and do the same thing. We're obviously too shallow in the atmosphere, and they've been able to track us well enough to drop mines in our path, but luckily not enough for a missile lock, or we'd be dead already."

"Call it, XO," I say, every word feeling like a chore as I fight the control yoke to keep our abused ship from careening off course.

"Ten-degree dive, now," she says, her voice reverting back to the professional detachment of a naval officer under stress.

I comply, pushing the yoke forward until my console says we're at a ten-degree down angle aimed deeper into Big Ben's swirling clouds of noxious gases. A few seconds later, what looks like rain starts to pelt the forward viewscreen, though I know little of it is actual water—more likely, it's the liquid states of the gases all around us.

"Hull stress estimated at sixty percent," Lin says as if she's reading a daily weather report. "Any further down, and we may start to buckle the hull plates. You know, assuming the mines didn't already do that."

"If they did, we'd certainly know about it by now. But we're still breathing," I say in reply. Regardless, she's right; we can't risk going any deeper into the atmosphere, so I level off the ship. Luckily for us, the explosions have stopped, though now we have another problem.

"They won't leave any time soon," Jessica says what we're both thinking. "They know we're here, and they won't trust that those mines got us."

"Any damage?" I ask, dreading the answer.

Which, surprisingly, comes from Harris. Or maybe not, since the seat he habitually fills is next to the damage control console. "Looks like a failed pressure seal in the cargo hold and some minor damage to one of the drive exhaust nozzles, but the AI is saying that it's nothing to worry about, just to have a licensed StarHauler technician examine and repair it at our next scheduled service appointment. Do you want me to schedule it?"

I would look back at him in exasperated incredulity if I wasn't fighting so hard just to keep us on course and from going any deeper.

"What are you talking about?" Kayla asks, her tone mirroring my thoughts.

"Uh," Harris answers, "it's what's here on the screen. The AI wants to know if we want to go ahead and make an appointment with a licensed repair shop."

"No, we don't want to make an appointment!" Jessica yells from the co-pilot seat. "Just tell us if anything else breaks!"

"Uh, OK," he answers, and I feel genuinely bad for the guy. He's completely out of his element, though to be fair, I'm still trying to figure out what the guy's element actually is. What *does* he do when he's not dressing and putting makeup on other people? I know Owen used him as some sort of tech guru as well—at least when it came to the explosive implant he put in Jessica's neck, which is still there, by the way, albeit dormant—but that seemed more like a side gig for Harris.

"OK," I say to stop the parade of hits on my newest crew member—well, my only crew member besides Jessica. "A broken pressure seal isn't that bad, but we got lucky. None of those mines came particularly close; if they had, our little freighter would be a permanent addition to Big Ben's atmosphere."

"Or they don't want to kill us, just force us back to high orbit so they can capture us," Jessica says, and she's probably right; that many mine hits should have blown us to bits. The intensity must be dialed way down.

"But we can't stay down here for long," Jessica says, "or we'll lose enough hull integrity that we won't even be spaceworthy."

She's right. We're in trouble either way right now. "Commander Lin," I say, "now would be a really good time for you to come up with another crazy plan."

I can feel her glare even if I can't afford to turn my head to see it. But she doesn't object, and I let her think while I continue to fight the controls.

Finally, she speaks. "Sorry, sir, I've got nothing."

Uh oh.

"Anyone else have any bright ideas?" I ask Kayla and Harris.

"I think we should just surrender," Kayla surprises me by saying. "It's better than death, right?"

I ignore her because she's wrong. One of the first things they teach you about anti-pirate operations in the Promethean Navy is that you *never* let yourself get captured. You fight to the death. Pirates aren't exactly known for their ethics on the subject of torturing prisoners, sometimes just for fun.

But because no one has any useful ideas, that means it's up to me to figure something out. We're so dead...again.

Then it's like a little light goes on in the recesses of my brain. This happens to me sometimes when I'm under stress, and all hope seems lost. It's like when I was in high school, and I had left an assignment until the last minute, and I pulled an all-nighter and wrote a pretty good two thousand-word essay on early human expansionism through the lens of early post-diaspora video games. Sometimes, I do my best work under pressure. Plus, at that point, I was an *expert* on video games.

"OK," I say, tearing my eyes off my instrument readouts just long enough to look Jessica in the eyes. "Here's what we're going to do."

CHAPTER 14

Escape and Evade

Fifteen minutes later, we're ready to implement my truly daring plan. And I say daring because I'm sick of calling every plan we come up with stupid and foolhardy. But it's all of those things, maybe even more. The last time we had to fight off a superior foe in space, our ship actually had weapons and armor and that sort of thing. Wanderer, for all her charm, is a simple freighter. And that pirate ship above us is a bonafide warship, which means I put our chances of this working at less than twenty percent.

"In three, two, one, now!" Lin counts down, and I pull back on the control yoke, sending us upward at a fifteen-degree angle while she pours more power into the main drive—not enough to reignite the atmosphere around us as we did before, but enough, hopefully, to break free of Big Ben's gravity.

Slowly but inexorably, the altitude numbers on my console start to tick upward. It takes another thirty minutes, but the gas in front of us dissipates, revealing scattered stars as we break free of the atmosphere.

Then, something occludes those stars as the pirate ship comes roaring downward to intercept us.

"Execute phase two...now!" Lin cries, and I poke a command button on my console's touchscreen that cuts out the main drive, then uses the thrusters to flip *Wanderer* end over end. It takes longer than normal, even with the scant air resistance at this altitude, but it still works. As soon as we're showing our engine exhaust to the pirate vessel, I jam the throttle forward again, stopping short of full power so I hopefully don't ignite the atmosphere like we did before.

"They're following!" Lin calls out as *Wanderer* skims above the upper reaches of Big Ben's gas clouds. The timing on this needs to be perfect, so I keep my eyes on my console and don't acknowledge her statement.

An alarm warns of an energy buildup within the attacking ship—I'm actually surprised our little freighter's scanners have that capability—and I use our thrusters to juke to the left just in time to miss a laser blast that comes way too close for comfort. A pithy remark about close shaves flashes through my head, but I wisely hold my tongue. I can only hope the sensor scatter caused by the gas giant is enough to keep them from getting missile lock, or we're really dead.

Just at the right moment, I push forward on the control yoke, angling my ship down and deeper into the upper atmosphere. I reach my desired altitude and maintain it for a little while. We can't see the pirates anymore; the same sensor scatter that's keeping us largely hidden from them is doing the same to us. But the last view showed them still hot on our tail and making a descent to stay behind us. And I'm praying they're still close enough on our tail to *see* us.

"Be ready!" Lin shouts unnecessarily; I'm watching a counter tick down on my console, the numbers turning from yellow to red as they near zero. When they reach it, I jam the yoke forward again and dive my ship. But this time, I take a much steeper angle. It's a huge risk but a calculated one. And for a moment, we are diving straight down into the heart of Big Ben. But then, slowly but surely, we pull out of the dive and loop back upward. For a second, our engines labor to take us on such a steep up angle, and I push the throttles to the max, igniting the atmosphere around me but pushing us just hard enough to win against gravity's unforgiving embrace and hopefully escape before the flames engulf us.

"Explosion! And another!" Lin calls out. We can't actually see the explosions, but we can *hear* them reverberating through our hull, conveyed via the planet's thin atmosphere, though the sound is much farther away—more like distant thunder—than when the mines nearly hit us before.

"Yes!" I cry out in triumph. I want to pump my fist, too, but I don't dare take even a single finger off the controls.

Once again, the roiling gases in front of us give way to stars and the big dark of space. By letting the pirates see and chase us earlier, we'd taken a very large risk, but we also had a pretty good idea of where their minefield was, having gone through it earlier ourselves. And we led them straight into it, diving out of the way at the last moment. Apparently, they didn't see our dive quickly enough and blundered right into at least two of their own mines.

But my triumph ends quickly as the rear cameras clearly show the pirate ship emerging from the gas giant only slightly off angle in their pursuit of us, though it does appear that part of their ship is venting atmosphere. I guess I shouldn't be surprised they're still behind us; after all, *we* survived the minefield. It's a miracle it did them any damage at *all*.

I curse just as Lin also uses another word I've never heard from her before.

"What now?" she asks, her voice still blessedly professional despite our near-certain impending doom.

We can't go back to the gas giant, not with that pirate between us and it, and regardless, we've already proven that approach won't work. So, our options are getting extremely limited…as in die now or die in a few minutes.

"We're too far off course to get to Carter's World," I say, still refusing to accept that I might die a second time in the last few weeks, and for *real* this time, "but maybe we can lose them in the gas giant's rings?" I phrase it as a question on purpose; flying as fast as we are through the rings of a planet is tantamount to suicide. All it takes is a few small rocks impacting our hull at speed to put holes in us.

"I think I'm going to be sick," Kayla says from behind me as I hear her frantically undoing her restraints and then running from the cockpit.

I look at Lin, and she shrugs. "I can't think of anything better," she replies, though I know she's also fully aware of the foolishness of the desperate plan, "and we should be able to get there just ahead of them."

I set in the new course and start praying in earnest, because religious or not, it's time to cover *every* base.

Two minutes later, however, Jessica cries out in surprise.

"What?" I demand, checking my console for any clue as to what shocked her. The last thing we need right now is an engine burnout or even a single thruster going offline.

"They're losing acceleration and changing vector!" she exults. "They're turning, breaking off pursuit!"

"Huh," I say in confusion. "Maybe we damaged them more than we thought?"

Jess is shaking her head but smiling ear to ear now. "Who cares, as long as they're not chasing us."

I nod in agreement. "OK. Lay in a course for Carter's World, full burn. Let's get on the right vector and get far away before they change their minds."

CHAPTER 15

Meeting the President

I t's the dead of night on the part of the planet where Kayla directs us to land. We can't go straight to the capital city and meet with her father in the presidential mansion. According to her, they think some of the local populace may actually be working with the pirates, spying for them on the planet's surface. That seems farfetched at first, given the small size of the population and their common ancestry and tight family ties, but she explains that they get a good share of migrant farm workers that come to the planet only during certain regional seasons. A spy could easily hide among their number.

Still, it feels somehow wrong to meet with a planetary president on a dark piece of farmland with a single small house and a surprisingly large barn, big enough to accommodate our ship. We land on one of the plowed fields, almost breaking off our landing gear in the process, but then taxi slowly into the barn, directed by a man on the ground.

As Jessica and I do the post-landing checklist to shut everything down, Kayla is quite literally bubbling over with excitement at seeing her father. As soon as the ship stops in the barn, she jumps out of her seat and leans forward, kissing me on the cheek, and then bounds out of the cockpit to go open the airlock for us to disembark.

Chagrined, I look over to see Jessica frowning at me. "Really, Brad?" she asks. "Can we at least *try* to be professional?"

I shrug, embarrassed but also a little annoyed at her tone. Who is she to tell me who I can and can't date, especially since she's made it pretty clear she doesn't want to be with me?

I don't say any of that, of course. Paula Mendoza may have raised a screwup and eventual mass murderer, but even I'm not *that* stupid. I *was* married, after all.

Harris excuses himself from the cockpit next, mumbling something about changing his shirt. Judging by his usual appearance, he'll probably exchange one rumpled t-shirt for another and look equally dodgy in front of President Carter. But I don't say anything; he might put makeup on me in my sleep.

Right as I'm about to get up and leave as

well, Jessica stops me. "Hold up," she says, her condescending tone from before lost. "Before we go out there, I don't think we should blindly trust Kayla and her father. We got away from that pirate way too easily."

"You call that easily?" I ask incredulously. "We almost died like six times!"

She rolls her eyes at me. "You know what I mean. No way a couple of those mines injured them enough to stop chasing us unless one was a *really* lucky hit. Something about this entire situation seems off to me. Just promise me we won't take everything they say at face value. Even if they're honest with us, there may be more going on here than even they know."

I'm hoping this is just her jealousy of my budding relationship with Kayla. However, despite only knowing Jessica for a few weeks, I'm already certain she wouldn't stoop to throwing suspicion at another woman, even if she is *jealous*, which I'm also pretty sure she isn't. "OK," I tell her, "We'll be careful."

We both strap on the pistols we took from Owen Thompson and his team and head out of the cockpit and to the airlock, where Kayla has already opened the hatch and extended the ladder.

I let Lin climb down first, and when I follow, I find a circle of three men facing me and the ship. Kayla is in the arms of the older man in the middle, apparently her father. He's hugging her tightly and talking in her ear; it actually looks a little too intimate for a father-daughter, but hey, this is a backwater world; maybe they do things differently out here in the sticks.

The president releases his daughter and extends a hand to shake mine. I step forward and take it, receiving a firm handshake that squeezes my hand just a little too tightly.

"Captain Lopez," the president says in a deep baritone through a salt and pepper beard—we agreed prior to landing we would use our false names; no use having the *entire* Fringe knowing who we really are, and Kayla agreed, "I want to thank you for returning my daughter to me and coming to help us. I know our plight seems desperate, and it is, but every little bit helps."

I nod in reply, but it's Lin who speaks first from our side. "President Carter, it's a pleasure to meet you, but do you mind introducing us to your friends?"

I'm worried for a second that the president will take offense, but he smiles and motions to the man at his left. "This is Wesley Adamson, my chief of staff and most trusted advisor. And this," motioning to the shorter, stockier man at his right, "is Norman Smith, the head of our planetary militia. At my orders, they are the only two men who know of your arrival here today. The rest of my cabinet, advisors, and what's left of our militia and police forces will only be told if they need to know. That way, we don't risk tipping off the pirates."

I study the two men. Adamson has a shifty look about him, like he's cheating at poker—classic politician. Smith is short and burly and has a hard look, more so than I would expect from a simple farm planet's militia leader, but maybe understandable given he's lost most of his fighting force to pirates in the last year.

Jessica frowns. "That's a good plan, sir, but we're afraid the pirates are already tipped off that we're here. We had a run-in with one of their ships in the outer system, which almost ended very poorly for us."

Carter frowns back and nods. "Yes, Kayla was telling me about that. I'm sorry it happened. But luckily, we've had a few smugglers brave enough to run the blockade to bring us medical and other off-world supplies at exorbitant prices. So we're hoping the pirates will just assume you're another of those."

Jessica is clearly unconvinced but doesn't respond, giving me a chance to finally butt in. "Let's hope so, but let's not count on it. We should get down to business quickly before they have a chance to regroup and think too hard about things. But first, is there somewhere we can get a cup of coffee? We're all running on fumes right now."

"Yes, of course," the president says, turning to his chief of staff. "Wesley, why don't you take them into the farmhouse and get them situated while I catch up with my daughter? Norman, go with them; they can start quizzing you on the situation if I'm not there when they're ready."

We follow the two other men out of the barn and across the yard to the little house we saw from the air. It has cheery orange light coming from the windows and reminds me a bit of my grandparents' farmhouse on Denton III, which instantly makes me feel simultaneously homesick and comforted. But I can see from the frown on Jessica's face that she's still worried about this entire situation. Well, Jessica is a worrier, that's for sure, though I promise myself I'll at least think about her concerns. After I get some coffee in me.

CHAPTER 16

Roundtable

"**A**nd that's the long and the short of it," Norman Smith finishes his monologue. We've been sitting with him, President Carter, and Adamson for the last two hours, talking through the pirate threat while we fight to stay awake.

"And you're sure there are only the two ships?" I ask dubiously.

He nods. "Absolutely sure. We may not have much in the way of a planetary sensor network, but we do know where the pirate base is—it's not like they've felt any need to hide it from us—and we keep everything we have pointed at it. We've only ever seen the two ships coming and going."

I nod, but I still have my doubts. The pirates must expect that the planet is watching their base, and underestimating even a ragtag pirate gang—

which this one certainly is not—can be extremely dangerous.

"We saw the one ship. What's the other one?" Jessica asks from the chair to my left. Kayla has planted herself to my right and moved her chair uncomfortably close, and I'm trying hard not to let it distract me.

"We've gotten a good sensor picture," Norman says with the first hint of excitement in the conversation, pushing a pad across the kitchen table with an image on it; apparently, the people of Carter's World don't use their implants for a lot of things, assuming they even have them.

I look at the picture of the ship on the screen and whistle. "Koratan corvette," I say, shaking my head. How come it's always Koratan ships trying to kill me? "No wonder they took out your patrol boat easily. Those things are no joke." It's true; the ship I'm looking at probably last saw actual naval service five decades ago, but it appears to be well-maintained and well-armed, and the pirates have no doubt updated it, given what we saw of the other ship that chased us. I still can't believe such a well-equipped pirate gang is so intent on claiming a planet as small and worthless as this one.

Norman shrugs. "You would know better than me, Captain Lopez. All we know is that these two ships are enough to shut down trade almost entirely in the system. We can barely find smugglers anymore willing to run the blockade to bring us goods, and those we *can* find, we can't afford."

"You're a farming planet, so you should have plenty of food; what goods are you trying to get?" Jessica asks, and I want to groan. Leave it to a wealthy city girl to have no understanding of economics or what it takes to live in a backwater like this. Of course, my understanding isn't much better, but at least it extends to the things I used to hear my grandparents talk about at their farm on Denton III.

President Carter is the one to answer, and he doesn't seem offended by her question. "You're right, Miss Kim. We have plenty of food—a surplus, really, since we export most of what we grow— but we don't have manufacturing for basic goods, medicines, and other things that our people need to live. My advisors estimate that we have three months left before we start to see some easily cured but truly nasty diseases start to ravage the planet. But the pirates won't even let the necessities through. We have to put an end to it for the good of my people."

That sounds like a terrific campaign speech to me, but I largely ignore it. I'm still studying the image of the Koratan corvette. It's a little smaller than *Persephone* and probably would have presented my old frigate with a fairly even fight. My old battlecruiser, *Lancer*, would have been able to swat it out of space with barely a thought. But it's still a significant bit of firepower for this far out in the Fringe, so far away from any of the big star nations. It's no wonder the Carter Worldians... Carterians... Carterans... whatever...haven't been able to find anyone willing to risk taking it on.

"When do you expect them to show up for their next raid?" Lin asks. I've let her do most of the talking in this conversation, leaving me to absorb the information and maintain a bit of command separation from the 'civilians'. She takes to it naturally, as any good XO does, and I marvel at how easily we can always find a rhythm with each other in situations like this. Too bad we'll obviously never have the opportunity to find a similar rhythm in our personal lives.

"Tomorrow, if they hold to their usual schedule," Norman, the militia guy again, answers Jessica's question. "Should be right around lunchtime that they show up."

"Great," I say, drawing a few startled glances. "That gives us just enough time."

"For what?" President Carter asks.

"For Harris here," I motion to the man, who fell asleep with his head on the table an hour ago and now startles awake as I say his name, "to make me look like a different person and for you to get me onto your orbital station."

Now, they're all looking at me in confused silence, including my own crew. I just grin and pick up one of the tea cakes they set out with the coffee and take a big bite. They're quite good, and I chew around my grin, enjoying their flabbergasted stares.

CHAPTER 17

I'm Going to Murder Harris

"Harris," I say through my comm bud, "when I told you to make me unrecognizable, this isn't exactly what I had in mind."

"Sorry, Captain," he replies in my ear, "You asked, and I delivered. I think it's perfect."

I frown. "You know how we talked about giving you a rank in our organization? Well, I *was* thinking petty officer, but I think you just convinced me to make you a spacer second class instead."

"That's good, right?" he asks somewhat eagerly. "Second class sounds better than petty."

Jessica breaks into our conversation. "Just ignore him, Harris. I think you did a marvelous job. And Brad, don't complain; you look beautiful." She's trying to joke around, but there's an undercurrent of stress in her tone.

I command my implant to change the comm to Lin's private channel. "You OK?"

"Sure," she answers shortly. "Why wouldn't I be? I'm the one safe behind a locked door, while you're the one being an idiot."

Ouch. She wasn't happy when I first presented my plan, and she hasn't really warmed up to it in the half day since. And when Jessica is annoyed with me, she becomes Confident Lin, the stern XO who doesn't pull her punches with anyone, much less her captain. Most of the time, I like Confident Lin, but not when she's angry at me.

"It'll be fine," I say with false casualness. "At least Harris got one thing right: I don't look *anything* like myself right now."

She grunts in reply. "I still think we should have done more intel gathering before we launched *any* operation."

"Come on," I say, "this operation is all about intel gathering. What better way to get information on the pirates than to get up close and personal? Speaking of which, our guests have arrived, so I'd better go."

I cut off the comm channel before she can reply and call me an idiot again and turn my attention to the guy who just walked into the small café on Carter's World's orbital platform. He's definitely a pirate. In fact, if you were to ask a fourth grader to draw you a pirate, he'd probably draw this guy. Not only does he have the stereotypical mohawk haircut, but every square centimeter of his exposed skin that *isn't* covered by tattoos seems to be hosting multiple very painful-looking piercings. Some of them look downright impossible, and I can't figure out how he eats. Heaven forbid he should ever try to kiss anyone or even blow his nose. A hard sneeze would probably kill him.

He walks in with the swagger and confidence of a guy who knows there's no one nearby to challenge him. He's wearing black leather pants and a mesh tank top underneath a matching leather jacket, and he has a shotgun held lazily in one hand and propped up against his shoulder. He looks ridiculous but also very scary. Like, I might laugh at him, but he'd definitely kill me for doing so.

Since I'm sitting near the café entrance, he looks at me first and swaggers over to my table.

"Hey, sweetheart," he says with a lewd smile. "Whatcha got for me under that dress?"

I shy away from him, pretending that I'm intimidated. But I'm really just uncomfortable. My pantyhose is riding up something fierce! How do women wear these things? And the high heels hurt *so* bad. Again, I silently curse Harris for disguising me to look like a woman. What was he thinking?

And why didn't I put a stop to it before it got started? Morbid curiosity, I guess.

"Come on, sweetheart," the man says as he leers at my chest; I wonder what he would think if he knew those were just rolled-up socks. "Give us your name at least."

Ugh. He's not going to give up; I can see it in his eyes and the way he undresses me with them. Is this really how women are constantly being looked at by men? I suddenly feel guilty on behalf of my entire gender.

"Kiki," I say in a falsetto voice, giving the first name that comes to mind, which I immediately regret. Kiki? Really? Could it sound any more fake? But apparently, the guy likes what he hears because he slips into the seat across from me, ignoring the other patrons in the café.

"Listen, girly," he says, giving his best toothy smile that clearly demonstrates he's never met a dentist and makes some of his piercings stretch the skin in ways that make me want to puke a little. I want to kick him in his happy place under the table, but I refrain. "What's say you and I go somewhere a little more private? I might even let you keep that fancy jewelry afterward."

OK, now I'm literally going to murder Harris. He thinks I won't, I bet, but I *am* a mass murderer. I don't know why people keep forgetting that. They should be *way* more afraid of me than they are.

"I can't. I'm married," I say. Ugh, if this doesn't work, I *will* kick the guy.

He frowns but then seems to suddenly remember where he is and why he's actually here. He reaches out and grabs my left hand, roughly removing the fake diamond ring Harris put there. At least, I hope it's fake; if it's not, I'm going to have some serious words with my newest spacer second class.

After that, the big pirate empties out the purse I brought, finding the seventy-three credits we put in there for this exact purpose and shoving it in a bag with the ring. After that, he gets up and moves past me to start hassling the couple at the next table over. But as he does so, he paws my fake chest a bit as he roughly yanks the—hopefully also fake—pearl necklace off my neck. Then he's gone.

"Harris," I whisper into my comm. "You're a dead man."

"What?" he asks. "Did it not work?"

I don't answer; let him stew in uncertainty.

"He's kidding, right? Captain likes to joke around, right?" I can hear him asking Lin over the open comm as I try to subtly keep an eye on the pirate who accosted me, along with a few of his buddies outside the café shaking down people in the station's small concourse and the shops circling it.

As I watch, one across the way gropes a pretty blond girl, making her scream. When her husband or boyfriend tries to put himself between the pirate and the girl, he ends up on the ground with a broken jaw for his trouble. I itch to jump to my feet and intercede, but that would defeat the purpose for which I'm here today, which is just to watch, listen, and learn as much as I can about the foe we now face.

Unfortunately, knowing that I can't help those around me—that doing so now would rob my ability to help them later when it really counts—doesn't translate to feeling one iota better about that fact. So I watch, and I fume, and my hand twitches at my side for the pistol that isn't there.

The tattooed and pierced pirate finishes stealing everything he can from the café's customers and owner and then leaves out the front door. I watch his back as he goes and try to memorize everything about him so I can remember to shoot him the next time I see him.

CHAPTER 18

A Gift from the Admiral

A half day later, I'm back in the tiny farmhouse where Wanderer is still hidden in the nearby barn. We hitched a ride to and from the capital city in the aircar belonging to Norman Smith, the militia leader, and then used the one-operating public shuttle to get to and from the orbital station itself.

I'm still fuming, and I had some truly choice words for Harris about the disguise he put me in. But then Jessica stepped in and reminded me that, as *captain*, I could have simply ordered the man not to do it. Stupid Lin and her stupid logic. In the end, I grudgingly apologize to Harris for yelling at him while my XO watches like the schoolteacher who made me apologize for kicking my bully in the groin in fifth grade.

I also feel like I need to apologize to every woman I

see, but I haven't had a moment alone with either Lin, who rode with me and Harris to and from the orbital, or Kayla, who stayed behind on the farm with her father. Not that I would know what to say anyway. 'Hey, I'm sorry for being a man. We all really suck. Please forgive us.' Yeah, real smooth.

So, I'm a bit grumpy when we sit down for another annoying strategy session with President Carter and his two advisors, this time in the farmhouse's tiny living room.

"What did you learn?" the president asks without preamble. Maybe he's just a no-nonsense guy generally, but his clipped tone could also have something to do with his short-short-wearing daughter sitting so close to me on the small couch that it's hard to tell where I end and she begins. I even try to move aside at one point, casually, but she just follows right along, and now she has an iron grip on my hand.

I really need to find time alone with her so I can somehow talk her out of all this. Assuming I really want to, which I'm pretty sure I do, but maybe there's a voice of doubt in my head. After all, Lin has made it abundantly clear that she and I are never meant to be. Would it be so bad to move on?

I'm so confused, though that's nothing new for me, I guess.

"We learned that the pirates don't operate as a unit," I say both to answer the president's question and distract myself from Kayla's other hand, now rubbing my back. "The ones I saw were disorganized and operated as individuals the entire time. I even saw a few folks on the station get shaken down by two or even three different pirates because they weren't even coordinating sections of the station to loot. How did it go on the ground?"

It's the president's chief of staff, Wesley Adamson, who answers. He's the one who was at the presidential mansion in the capital city while Carter was here with Kayla—I thought it was odd the president would send an advisor to take the heat, but apparently, Adamson insisted.

"They were upset the president wasn't there," he tells us. "But they still walked in like they owned the place. And after all the artwork they stole and loaded into their ship, they pretty much do. We couldn't pay their tribute in cash—no surprise there—but their leader, Poulter, said that we'd better have the money next time, with interest. And that was *after* he emptied the treasury vault of every scrap and credit we had, both the physical and digital."

President Carter frowns. "Next time, they won't be so generous. I have a feeling this is our last warning before things truly escalate. Captain Lopez, we'll need to move as quickly as we can."

I get his desire to do things fast, but they've been

under these pirates for almost a year! Can't this guy be patient for a few more weeks?

Norman Smith takes his turn to speak up. "We shouldn't try and take them again on the planet's surface. Trying that with our militia was a mistake. We can't fight against their air support. That corvette isn't capable of atmospheric flight, but their smaller ship is, as we learned painfully last time."

I nod. All this I know, but I still haven't figured out a way to defeat our enemies. I need more time to think about it. Unfortunately, Jessica and I were both naval officers, not Marines, and even the ground assaults we did participate in as junior officers were planned and usually run by the gunnery sergeants while everyone *pretended* we were really in command.

"Even if we could fight them again with the militia," Norman is saying, "I doubt we could get more than a dozen of our people to show up. They're not professional soldiers, and they've been spooked by the eighty percent casualty rate of the last try."

"What if we could arm them better than the last time?" Jessica asks right before I can. We're on the same page.

Norman shrugs. "It would have to be a pretty good set of weapons to get them to leave their farms and go up against a serious foe again."

Honestly, anything would be better than the two-hundred-year-old bolt-action hunting rifles the militia normally uses. A big caliber hunting rifle with a kick like a mule *feels* like real power in your hands until you face down a guy with a laser or projectile assault rifle who can put a hundred rounds into you in seconds. Then you feel awfully small.

Not that I have any direct experience being the guy with the bolt-action rifle, but there were a couple of times I was commanding part of the guys with the assault rifles, so I can sort of imagine what the other side was feeling.

"Let me ask you something, Mr. Smith," I say. "How many militia members *could* you raise in a pinch, assuming we had the right weapons?"

He shrugs, which doesn't fill me with confidence. "I still doubt I could get more than two dozen, and even that would require that they *really* be the right weapons." His pessimism is starting to wear on me a bit. I mean, it's not like we're facing impossible odds and don't have a plan; well, yes, it is, but his defeatist attitude isn't helping.

I stand up, extricating myself from Kayla's grasp. "Well, let's go see what goodies are in my ship's hold."

In the excitement of our daring escape from the pirates, followed by the quick trip to and from the orbital to observe our foe in action, I'd pretty much forgotten all about the crate Admiral Walters had ordered put into our cargo hold. We head there now to check it out.

True to the admiral's promise, the crate unlocked once its internal nav chip verified we were in Carter's System. All it needs to open is my fingerprint. I only hope that the gases that got past our cargo hold seals in the atmosphere of Big Ben didn't damage the contents, but it all looks intact from the outside.

Without any hesitation or fanfare, I open the thing and peer inside.

I freeze, unable to believe what I'm seeing, but feeling a surge of hope for the first time since we started this impossible mission. Admiral Walters has given us some real toys to play with. And with them, we actually stand a chance.

CHAPTER 19

Two and a Half Samurai

"**I** can see why she didn't want us opening the crate while we were still in Republic space," Lin observes as we study the contents, which are now laid out in neat rows across the floor of our otherwise empty cargo bay. I grunt my agreement. With the arsenal now before us, we could start a revolution on most planets and probably win one on a small planet like Carter's World. And the pirates won't stand a chance against us if we can find enough people to wield the weapons.

In all fairness, it almost disappoints me. Not that I *enjoy* impossible missions, but daring and risky plans that somehow defy the odds have sort of become a thing for me and Jessica since we met. I expected this mission to top all of them, assuming it didn't kill us. But now, it just seems so *easy*.

Except for one thing: even with an array of weapons like these, they're all infantry or Marine arms. There's nothing that can help us take out either of the pirate ships. Especially that corvette. And our unarmed freighter isn't going to be any help in that department either.

"OK," Norman the militia guy says, rubbing his hands together like a kid in a candy store. "With this, maybe I can get you twenty-five troops. What's the plan?"

The plan. Yeah. Having one of those would be nice right now.

"Norman, have you ever seen a movie called *Seven Samurai*? It's an Old Earth classic." It was also my grandpa's favorite movie.

He shakes his head, looking confused.

"We're your seven samurai," I continue. "Well, two and a half if we're generous in how we count Harris. But the bottom line is, we're going to train and equip what's left of your militia to make those pirates run for the hills."

"Uh, we want them out of our system, not in our hills," he says, his eyebrows knit together.

I sigh. This guy really isn't any fun at all. "It's just an expression, Norm. We'll kick them out of the system. Happy?"

He nods doubtfully, but at least he walks off to start calling in some of his militia members.

Jessica steps up to me once he's out of earshot. "You don't have a plan yet, do you?"

I shake my head. "Nope. I was hoping *you* might."

She laughs at me and shakes her head right back. "Nope. Sorry, sir. Fresh out." It's another joke like the one about me making a beautiful woman; that's *two* in as many days. I'm slowly wearing her serious disposition down.

"Harris," I call to my spacer second class, who is staring at the weapons like they're foreign objects.

"Yeah, boss?"

"How about you? You have a plan?"

He looks at me for a moment, probably trying to figure out if I'm serious. Then he shrugs. "Owen used to always say, 'Take the fight to the enemy'. I never really knew what that meant, but he sure said it a lot."

I wasn't really listening to Harris—I didn't expect him to say anything constructive—but now I focus my full attention on him. "Say that again, Spacer," I demand.

"Uh, take the fight to the enemy."

"Harris, you're a genius. And you just got promoted to spacer first class!"

He looks over at Jessica in confusion. "Wait, I was a spacer second class, now I'm a first? Isn't one lower than two in the Navy?"

My XO just rolls her eyes at him. "Come on, Harris," she says, "let's get some lunch, and I'll explain naval ranks to you…again." They head through the internal hatch that leads to *Wanderer's* passenger area.

About that time, Norman walks back into the hold from outside. "I got five people already to say yes once I told them what we can equip them with. I should have another twenty by later today. They're coming from all over the planet, so they can be here in, say, two days. That work?"

"It'll have to," I tell him. "It's not like we have any other options for ground troops."

He nods and rushes off to make more calls, and I start working on my plan.

CHAPTER 20

Caught Between Two Rocks

I t's ten at night local time, which means it's almost the start of a new day; whoever terraformed this rock didn't get the rotation speed right, so the day here is only twenty and a half hours long. Annoying.

I'm standing outside on the farmhouse's front porch after ending another four-hour discussion on tactics with Norman, during which I feel like I had to explain everything six times, which was particularly tough given I'm making it all up as I go. I'm exhausted, but I've been running ragged for days now, and I feel the overwhelming desire just to stand here and do nothing more than breathe in the scents of the surrounding farmland and forest. The smells here are different for sure, but they still remind me generally of my grandparents' farm on Denton III.

The creaking of the screen door behind me heralds the arrival of someone else. A pair of arms reaches around my waist, and someone hugs me from behind. Has to be Kayla, unless Jessica suddenly decided to throw out her principles.

Kayla releases me and moves to stand beside me, and the scent of loamy soil and pine needles is replaced by the smell of lavender soap. I look down. Her hair is wet, and she's wearing pajamas. It all adds to the homey feeling. And I have to say the worn cotton PJs look surprisingly good on her.

"Do you think we can win?" she asks me in an uncharacteristically small voice.

I consider the question for a moment, not wanting to answer too quickly so as to seem that I'm not taking her query seriously. "Yes," I say. "If the men and women Norman is gathering are as solid as he says, and if the pirates give us a week or two to train them, then I think we'll almost certainly win."

I can see her frown in the moonlight. "That's a lot of ifs."

Nodding, I keep studying the darkness of the tree line several hundred meters away across the fields. For a supposed farm, I sure haven't seen anyone working those fields while we've been here. I assume Carter sent them all away, or maybe he even owns the place himself, though it's strange it would be so far away from the capital, in an entirely different hemisphere.

"Brad," Kayla says, drawing my attention again, breaking the rules by using my real name. "Admiral Walters said something funny to me on *Dauntless* about you, and it's been bugging me."

Confused, I look down at her. "What'd she say?"

She frowns. "Something about you having some big secret that everyone wants, and something about a system called Gerty...Gerbon..."

"Gerson," I finish for her but realize instantly I probably should have just kept my mouth shut.

"That's the one!" she says excitedly. She puts an arm around me and leans into me, and the smell of lavender grows stronger with her hair now right below my face, and the wetness of it soaks through my t-shirt. "What," she continues, "could be so important in Gerson that everyone in the galaxy would be after it?"

On the surface, it seems like just an innocent question. And it most likely is. But it's not one I'm going to answer. "Listen, Kayla, Walters was probably just trying to talk me up and make me seem more important than I really am. Truth is, there's nothing in this head of mine that anyone wants. Trust me."

She looks up at me, and in a brief second in the moonlight, it looks like anger flashes in her pretty blue eyes, but I must have imagined it because she snuggles back into me and sighs. "Brad, tell me this is all going to work out."

I breathe in deep, savoring the smells of the forest and of Kayla, but when I let the breath go, it escapes as a sigh. "Kayla, all I can tell you is that we'll do our best. Aside from that, luck is going to play a pretty big role, as will good old Mr. Murphy if we're not careful. But I can promise our best effort to free your planet."

That seems to satisfy her because she says nothing else but just keeps hugging me there on that front porch as I gaze out over the fields. It starts to feel *really* good, and I'm trying to think of a polite way to extricate myself before I do something I might regret, when she looks up again. "Brad, I'm scared."

I reach up and put my arms around her, hugging her back lightly. "Nothing to be scared of," I lie. "Just some pirates. And we've got bigger guns."

"Let's leave. Now," she says, a sudden urgency in her voice. "We can get in your ship and fly away somewhere where there are no pirates and no worlds under siege. You can find Admiral Walters and sell her whatever information she thinks you have, and we can live off the money and just be together. Wouldn't that be wonderful, Brad?"

The sudden about-face from scared little girl to excited paramour has my head spinning, and I slowly push her away to look her in the eyes. "Kayla, think about what you're saying. What about your father? Would you just leave him here?"

"No," she says, then bites her lower lip and starts to tear up. I feel instantly bad. "But we could take him with us," she continues. "Maybe the pirates will leave once they realize we don't have anything more for them to take. But the thought of anything happening to you makes me…"

She throws herself back at me and hugs me tight, burying her face back into my chest, adding the wetness of her tears to my already-soaked shirt. I hold her like that for a long time, even though I know I shouldn't lead her on, but I have no idea how to get out of the embrace without being a jerk. She needs the comfort right now.

"Stay with me tonight." The invitation catches me off guard, and I look down in confusion to see she's craning her neck to look up at me.

"Uh…" I start to say, but my mind goes blank, and words fail me entirely. Slowly, I reach around and unwrap her arms from around my back and then take a step back from her. This time, I'm certain I see her eyes flash with anger, and her lower lip juts out in a healthy pout.

"Kayla, I'm not…" I try to say again, but I still can't form the words. Suddenly, she takes a step forward, grabs my head, and pulls it down, kissing me hard. Before I can even fight it, she releases me from the kiss and then steps back again.

"You know where to find me if you change your mind," she says coyly and then spins and walks back to the farmhouse door in a way that tells me she is one hundred percent sure I'm watching her go.

Then, as she reaches the darkened doorway, I see another person emerge from it: Jessica. The two women regard each other in a way that reminds me of two cats who used to fight all the time on Grandpa's farm, and then Kayla disappears inside, and Jessica steps out onto the porch.

"Uh," I say to Jessica because my brain has suddenly shut off...again.

She looks at me with a deep frown. "So, this is you being careful with trusting Kayla, huh?"

"I...uh...well...she kissed *me*," I stammer.

Jessica shakes her head in disappointment. "Brad, at least be man enough to admit that you like her."

"But...I..." I still don't know what to say. Because to any outside observer, I *should* like Kayla. She's cute, she's strong, and she clearly likes me. In fact, the only reason I can think of that I don't like Kayla is because I'm in *love* with Jessica. But I can't tell *her* that!

She shakes her head at me, grunts in frustration, and hisses something that sounds like 'men'. Then she storms off in the direction of the barn and our ship, leaving me standing there alone, trying to figure out how I've managed to drive off two women in one night without even trying. It might be a galactic record, and someone can send me a certificate that reads 'Humanity's Biggest Numbskull'.

I slowly walk in the same direction that Jessica just went, entering the huge barn and looking at my ship wedged inside. I stare at the ladder leading up to the airlock hatch, but I make no move toward it. Something tells me I should let Lin have the ship to herself tonight. Well, to her and Harris. He went to bed hours ago; there wasn't too much need for a makeup artist in our late-night tactics session, even though he was the one who provided me with the seed of the idea for our latest plan.

So, instead of walking toward the ship, I climb up a long wooden ladder to the hay loft high above, where I do something I haven't done since I was thirteen: I make myself a nest in the hay and lay down in it, ignoring it poking through my thin, still-wet shirt. There I lie, awake for at least another hour, turning the events of the evening over and over in my head until I finally slip into a fitful sleep without finding a single answer to why I'm such a monumental moron.

CHAPTER 21

Training Days

L uckily for me, Norman delivers the first sixteen of his hand-picked militia fighters a day early, and they start to arrive at the farm in small groups of two or three before I even wake up with the crowing of the rooster.

I find them all gathered, chatting excitedly, around the large table in the farmhouse's dining room. It's actually the biggest space in the small house, and it's perfect for a gathering like this, even though only about half of them can sit.

Almost to a person, they're in much better shape than I expected. When I think of a planetary militia, the image that usually comes to mind is a bunch of good ole boys with beer bellies, ball caps, and mullets who scream pig calls as battle cries. But not this group. They're lean and strong, and I can only guess got that way from hard work on the farms. But a few move in ways that remind me of Marines I've served with, and I have to upgrade my respect for Norman Smith's training methods. Maybe we can do this after all.

"This is Captain Ben Lopez," Norman introduces me as if I'm his best friend and his hand-picked savior. "He's a mercenary from off-world, "a few of them look at me a bit dubiously when he calls me a mercenary, "and is going to be leading our fight against the pirates. And he's got some surprises for all of you."

I try not to glare at him. I just got my first cup of coffee, and I haven't even had time to take a single sip. That, and I have hay in places no man should *ever* have hay, and it's the itchy kind. But I'm up, whether I like it or not, though I find myself wishing I had something a little stronger to put in my coffee this morning as my mind keeps going back to the events of last night.

"OK," I say to the gathered farmers-turned-militia-fighters. "You and the other nine people we're expecting are going to be the ones who drive these pirates off your planet and out of your system." I'm trying to sound inspiring, but it's early, and I just lost one, possibly two, loves of my life last night, so I come out sounding monotone. It doesn't matter. If they need me to inspire them to fight for their own planet, we've already lost.

"After breakfast," I tell them, "we'll head out

to the barn and my ship, where we'll get you outfitted with the finest off-world weapons you've ever seen. You're going to want to start using them immediately, but we're going to train you up Marine style, which means you don't even load them without my say-so." There are a few mutters at that, but they can deal with it. Despite first impressions, I don't yet trust any of them not to shoot themselves, or worse, me, in the foot.

"We believe we have two weeks before the pirates' next raid. By then, I promise that you'll be the most efficient killing machines that Carter's World has ever seen." That's a really low bar, but it seems to make them stand up a little straighter. "But only if you listen to and do *everything* I tell you. Clear?"

Well, they're not military, so instead of a perfectly timed chorus of 'Sir, yes sir', I get back a smattering of 'Sure', 'Yes', 'Why not?' and at least one 'I guess so'. It'll have to do.

Five minutes later—I've never seen a group that large eat so quickly—we're out in the barn, and I'm bringing out weapons from the external cargo bay hatch on my ship. I haven't seen Jessica or Kayla this morning yet, and I'm very much hoping that lasts long enough for the caffeine to take effect.

It doesn't; halfway through my handing out of assault rifles and a few other special toys Admiral Walters included, Jessica enters the cargo bay from the inner hatch and starts helping me distribute the weapons, all while not meeting my gaze even once. Fun.

I suppose it shouldn't upset me as much as it does. I know I'm not any kind of a catch. In fact, I think Jessica would be insane to love me back the way I love her. She's an intelligent, caring, brilliant supermodel, and I'm...well, Brad Mendoza. It would defy logic for the two of us to end up together. Not to mention, I've only known her a few weeks! But no amount of rational thought will banish the feeling in the pit of my stomach every time I look at her and the worry that I may have lost her before I even had a chance to win her.

I'm moping, even though I know I shouldn't be. I was a senior *captain* in the Promethean Navy! I once defeated a pirate fleet with a single battlecruiser. I received the King's Star *four times* for bravery and for service above and beyond. I liberated Jalisco from a rebel blockade for crying out loud! I was one of the youngest officers in Promethean Naval history to attain my rank, and I was married to the daughter of a fleet admiral— even though he hated me—and was the envy of the stupid dinner parties she used to drag me to.

There's no way I should be acting like a teenage boy whose first girlfriend just dumped him for the quarterback! I should have more confidence than this. I should...

But   no.   Because   while   all   of   those

accomplishments technically belong to me, I'm no longer the man who earned or deserved them. I'm Brad Mendoza, failure, murderer, drunk, and now...forever alone.

So, I do what any good officer does when his personal life is a mess. I take it out on the new recruits. And thus begins the worst two weeks of their lives, courtesy of the Butcher of Bellerophon.

CHAPTER 22

They All Hate Me

For thirteen days, I make every man and woman that Norman Smith has gathered learn to hate every ounce of my guts. I'm fairly certain that, at this point, each one of them would happily kill me without a moment's remorse. But they learn surprisingly fast, and I'm now also certain that we now have a fighting force that can liberate Carter's World from the pirate threat.

If only I could convince President Carter of how we need to use them.

Kayla hasn't been around much the last two weeks —she's been on the opposite side of the planet tending to her family's farm near the capital—and I'm grateful for that. I know I need to take her aside and explain to her that I don't feel about her the way she obviously does about me, but I'm also dreading the conversation. I'm a coward, sure, but most men are when it comes to disappointing a beautiful woman, even when you're as practiced at it as I am.

Unfortunately, I don't think President Carter got the memo that I rejected Kayla's attempt to get me into bed that night, because he's been especially cold to me these last two weeks. And when I finally share my daring and genius plan with him, he's more than a little upset.

"Let me get this straight; you want me to *surrender* myself to the pirates?"

I smile tightly as he puts my proposal into the worst wording possible. "No, Mr. President," I say, really trying and failing to keep the impatience out of my tone, "I want you to *pretend* you're giving yourself up to them. We need them to think we're truly desperate, and this will be the best way to put them at ease by making them think you've given up all hope."

"It's insane," he says, shaking his head and throwing his hands in the air. Next to him, his faithful little lapdog, Adamson, nods in agreement.

"Mr. President," Norman Smith soothes from beside me, "Captain Lopez has shared his plan with me, and I think we ought to give it a chance."

Carter scowls at his militia leader but nods grudgingly, and I feel relieved again that I was able to convince Norman to back me on this.

"It's really quite simple, Mr. President," I say, imbuing my voice with as much respect and deference as I can. "You've already made it clear that we can't fight the pirates in the capital or on the orbital where civilians can get caught in the crossfire, and inviting the pirates to meet us on a farm like this one would instantly make them suspicious. There's also no way we can fight them in space; my ship has no weapons, and you have no more patrol fleet. So, that leaves only one place in this entire system where we can fight them."

"Their base," he finishes for me, and even though I already told him that was the plan, I'm glad he's starting to see the logic in it, even unwillingly.

"Yes, their base. It has the triple advantage of being the place where they'll feel most secure and relaxed, of being the one place we can ensure we get all of them together, and finally, it's the only place we can fight them on the ground without risk of civilian casualties."

"Except risk to the president himself," Adamson argues from his boss's side. I ignore him.

"Isn't the risk to one man, no matter how important he may be, worth it to safeguard and liberate the lives of every other civilian in this system?" Jessica asks from beside me. We may not exactly be hanging out a lot right now in our spare time, but we're still in sync enough that we can rely on each other in conversations like this. And anything said in her upper-crust Promethean accent and perfect diction just sounds so much more noble than the usual drivel from my mouth.

And it works because President Carter starts to look thoughtful.

I'm opening my mouth to try and bring this thing home when I hear Kayla's voice behind me.

"Do it, Daddy," she says sternly, and I turn in surprise. I didn't even know she'd come back today. She's standing there, looking her father dead in the eye with a determined stare.

I look back at the president, and I can see the moment he folds.

"Fine, I'll do it. But it had better work," he levels a finger at me.

I nod but say nothing, as nothing more needs to be said.

"OK," Jessica says, "then let's talk logistics. The militia will ride in *Wanderer*; she's not rated for that many passengers, but for a simple in-system hop, she should have more than enough life support, and there's plenty of room in our hold. But because she's such a small ship, the pirates will never suspect we're bringing a small army with us."

"Uh, yeah," Norman says uncomfortably, "about that…"

CHAPTER 23

Cattle

D o you remember how I had that little sense of weird disappointment when I first opened that crate of weapons in Wanderer's hold and thought to myself how easy this would all be with them? I felt it robbed me of the chance to pull another classic Brad Mendoza and Jessica Lin super risky stunt where we snatch victory from the jaws of a pit bull...or something like that.

Well, if I had a time machine and could go back and meet myself from that moment two weeks ago, I'd shoot myself in the face. Because this just got a whole lot more complicated.

"You're joking," Jessica says.

"I'm not," Norman Smith answers. "It's true."

"And *how* did the pirates get a life sign scanner?" I ask as I massage my temples to try and stop the headache that's quickly forming there. I've been sober now for *way* too long.

He shrugs. "We're an agricultural planet. Even one bug or rodent brought in from another planet's ecology could be enough to wipe out our crops. So, we had it installed in our orbital to scan incoming ships and their crews. The pirates took it the first time they raided the station. We assumed it was so that they could sell it—the things are *really* expensive; took us decades of saving to get one—but it's possible they've kept it until now."

I shake my head. "You realize this changes *everything*, right?"

Norman looks apologetic but just nods in reply.

This is bad, really bad. No one can scan a moving ship for lifeforms; life sign scanners rely heavily on thermals, and there's simply too much heat that comes off a starship in operation for even the best sensors to see through all that. But when a ship stops...

"You understand," Jessica says, "that as soon as we land, they will know our cargo hold is full of people? They'll blow us off that asteroid they call a base before we can even get your men and women out through the airlock."

Norman frowns and just nods, clearly upset and a little embarrassed. Good; he should be.

"What if they don't think they're people?" a new

voice asks from the other end of the dining room table.

We all turn and look at the speaker, as if we can't believe Harris is actually talking in a planning meeting. He suddenly looks like a turtle trying to withdraw back into its shell.

"Harris," I bark, "if you have an idea, speak up. If it's a good one, I'll make you a petty officer."

He looks confused and glances over at Jessica.

"That's a good thing," she assures him. "A petty officer would be another jump in rank."

"Oh, ah, good. I guess. Anyway," he stammers, "what if the pirates think you have something else on board, like…" he trails off, and I can see he hasn't thought this through, but I wait him out anyway. "Like, I don't know, really big rodents?"

OK, giving him the time to think clearly wasn't helpful. But he is onto something.

"Cattle."

Now, everyone turns to look at me as if I just uttered something in a foreign language. "Look," I tell all the incredulous faces, "you've already said you don't have the money to pay him. But there are few things more valuable in space than fresh meat. Heck, I haven't had a steak in months. It might be enough of a draw, as stupid as it sounds, to make Poulter and his minions excited to let you come and visit."

I watch them all as they absorb this, and slowly, heads start to bob up and down. Kayla has moved up beside me and grabs my arm, and I can *feel* her beaming up at me. After the way Jessica has largely been looking at me the past two weeks, I have to admit I don't mind.

"OK," President Carter says. "I think we can round up some cattle."

CHAPTER 24

The Pirate King

To my surprise, the pirate leader, Poulter, agrees to the president's proposal to bring the next tribute payment to them. They've made no secret of the location of their base on a small rock in the system's asteroid belt. And I guess it appeals to their naturally lazy side to let their loot and victims come to them. They even seem a little excited at the prospect of the cattle.

We actually did round up some cattle, loading them onto one side of *Wanderer* out in the middle of a field in case the pirates had someone watching even way out here. But we parked close enough into the trees that we hope they couldn't see the cows get right *off* the ship through the opposite cargo hatch. Either way, it's the best we can do. And Norman and his troops get on the ship through that same tree-masked hatch.

Of course, a life sign scanner isn't just going to see a bunch of thermal signatures shaped like humans and think cattle. But it's Jessica who comes up with the plan for that part. Once Norman and his people are on board, all wearing vacsuits and carrying extra air bladders, she activates *Wanderer's* fire suppression system and fills the hold with fire retardant foam. Our hope is that the foam will act as insulation and muddy up the heat signatures enough that the life sign scanner's results will come back as inconclusive.

Now, I'm piloting *Wanderer* on the last leg to their base. With me in the cockpit are President Carter, Harris, and Jessica. I actually tried to get my XO to stay behind and run our 'ground support', but she saw through my overprotective suggestion and utterly refused. Harris just happened to already be in the cockpit when I got there, as if there was never any question he would be coming. The guy's brave; I have to give him that.

"Hey, little freighter," a snide female voice comes over the comm as we get close to the rock. "Land wherever you can find a spot, but don't scratch the paint on either of our ships, or we'll have your president's skull for a salad bowl."

"Lovely landing control," I quip because I'm nervous. No one laughs.

My only comfort is that down in my hold—Kayla was able to work her engineering magic and fix our broken pressure seal—are twenty-five of what I believe are now the best-trained militia fighters this side of the Jutzen Protectorate. Plus Norman, and he can hold his own.

A few minutes later, I'm setting my little ship down between the big—by comparison—corvette and the smaller but still heavily armed patrol ship that escorted us in for the last tense hour of transit. Moments after I set her down, a docking tube extends and mates with our starboard airlock, allowing us to access the underground base the pirates have carved out of solid rock, though why they went through all the trouble for a system like this one is still beyond me.

It's just President Carter and myself who make our way through the tube, leaving Jessica and Harris behind to mind the ship. When we arrive at the airlock at the other end, two pirates roughly frisk us from head to toe. I'm pretty sure the one who searched me now knows more about me than my proctologist ever did.

Finally deciding that neither of us has a missile launcher or nuclear warhead hidden in our body cavities, the two men let us through to the next hatch, which opens into a surprisingly comfortable-looking lounge.

I mean, they even have a bar setup at one end, and it looks like it's fairly well stocked. I haven't had a drink in almost a month now, and I'm surprised by how my eyes insist on seeking out all the old familiar labels and how my mouth is suddenly watering.

There's a big man sitting on, of all things, an overstuffed bean bag chair in the middle of the room. He's tall, and metal studs cover just about every square centimeter of his head-to-toe black leather clothing. Despite all the spikey metal, the two women, one to either side, cuddling up to him, don't seem to have yet been impaled. They're each a sight to see on their own. One has a nose ring with a chain leading down to her belly button. What happens if she needs to look up or turn her head? Ouch. The other has a mohawk and a bionic arm attached to the stub of where her real one used to be. Neither is what I would call exactly modestly dressed. They make Kayla's typical short shorts look positively prim.

"Ah, Carter," booms the big man. "I see you've finally come to your senses and brought my money. You'd better have the full payment this time."

This is perhaps the riskiest part of the plan because there are two of us, unarmed, and I count a dozen pirates, including the leader and his two groupies, in the room. And they are *all* armed. And we're about to tell them we don't have the full amount.

"Sorry, Captain Poulter," Carter says next to me without breaking the big pirate's gaze. I have to begrudgingly admit, the president is built of sterner stuff than I expected; his voice only trembles slightly. "We only have half, but we'll have the rest in a few weeks if you'll just let us trade some of our goods off planet."

The pirate captain, Poulter, grins wickedly, exposing teeth that have been filed to sharp points like a shark. I'd love to hear Harris critique this guy's look.

"What do you take me for, Carter? You think I'm going to let you go for help somewhere, or try to hire some kind of mercenary outfit? Like anyone you could afford would be able to scare me." The guy doesn't know just how on the nose he is.

"Besides," he rumbles, "I've seen that daughter of yours around. I think I'll just take the other half out of her."

Carter tenses next to me, and I put out a warning hand to stop him from reacting, though I can tell he's right on the edge.

"*Captain* Poulter," I say, emphasizing his title and trying my best to sound meek. "If I may?"

"Who is this worm?" sneers Poulter, still looking at Carter.

"He's my trade advisor," the president answers through clenched teeth.

"As we told you on our way in, I believe we have a deal that will make up for our little shortfall, at least temporarily," I say without waiting for permission, doing my best to make my voice sound a little more nasally like every bureaucrat always sounds to my ears. "Do you like ribeye?"

Poulter regards me for a moment and then surprises me by breaking out into a smile. "I do at that. And fresh meat sounds better than the canned stuff. Maybe we can deal, but I'll just keep that little Kayla in reserve. She might like to finally meet a real man."

To his credit, Carter doesn't openly react, but he's as tense as a spring in a car's shocks, ready to explode at any second. I speak up quickly.

"We brought twenty head of cattle in our ship's cargo hold. At current market prices off-planet, they're worth about a tenth of what we still owe you, but we're hoping the value of a fresh cut of meat will make it worth far more than that since we've brought it to you."

He frowns but nods slowly. "What do you think, girls?" he asks, looking down at each of his groupies in turn. The one with the interesting nose-to-belly chain sneers in our general direction, but the other just nods eagerly.

"Very well, let's see just how good these cattle look before I decide if little Kayla is going to come out here and live with me. I'll have my fresh meat one way or another."

Uh oh, that does it. Carter explodes, rushing

forward with a fist cocked. For an old guy, he moves pretty fast, but not fast enough. One of the other pirates lounging nearby, a tall guy with rings in places on his face I didn't know could support piercings—he makes the guy from the café look conservative—leaps out of his own lounge chair and clotheslines Carter before he even gets halfway to Poulter.

"Now, that was monumentally stupid," Poulter says in a low, menacing tone.

Then, pandemonium breaks out.

CHAPTER 25

Pandemonium

O n the flight in, Lin and I were able to capture some pretty good images of the pirate base. And we found what we were hoping for: a second entrance. Most places built underground have them. Otherwise, even the smallest cave-in would trap all the occupants inside with no hope of getting free.

And while we've been talking about cattle, steaks, and Kayla with Poulter and his merry crew, the rest of our passengers have been taking a long spacewalk around the backside of *Wanderer* and behind a short ridge to the other airlock into the base. And this is where Harris proves his worth. Because aside from being a makeup artist good enough to turn me into a woman, he was also Owen Thompson's tech guru. I find out later it takes him only twenty seconds to hack the airlock controls from the outside panel. Though I guess it's unlikely the pirates thought much about the possibility of a ground invasion and invested in a high-security lock.

Just as President Carter hits the ground and starts gasping for breath from the tall pirate's expert takedown, I spot movement in the mouth of a tunnel just behind and to the right of the bar. I leap down to the ground alongside the president, grateful that the artificial gravity inside the base makes me hit the floor quickly.

The sound of gunfire is deafening in the underground chamber, and so are the screams of the dying. We've taken the pirates completely by surprise, and few of them get off even a single shot before our boys and girls of the militia gleefully take them out.

About thirty seconds pass, though it feels much longer, before the last pirate slumps over with blood pooling on the front of his shirt. I wait another slow count of ten to make sure the battle is over, then I cautiously get to my feet and survey the carnage.

And it really is carnage. Those pirates that aren't dead are dying fast, and our militia boys and girls move in quickly and kick their guns away so that none of them will have a chance to avenge themselves with their last breaths.

My excitement at our successful ambush, however, fades when I turn my eyes to the beanbag chair at the center of the room, where I see the corpses of two women but no Captain Poulter. A quick count also reveals that we're one pirate short of what the room started with.

I swear loudly, and Norman Smith rushes to my side, his hair wet with sweat under the bubble helmet he's now removing from his head. "What's wrong?"

"Poulter got away!" I say louder than I intended. My ears are still ringing, but I hear Norman swear in response.

I look frantically around the room. I would have noticed if the big pirate had leapt over us to go down the corridor we entered from, and the only thing in that direction is the docking tube to our ship. But I scan the walls, searching until I find what I'm looking for.

The lounge is pretty gaudy, with sheets hanging from the walls like someone wanted to hide the bare rock or pretend they had tapestries or something. One of those sheets is moving now, swaying slowly back and forth. I sprint for it.

I think Norman is about to follow, but suddenly, more gunfire erupts. It seems the rest of the base's pirates have responded to the sound of the battle. Great.

That leaves me alone to follow Poulter to whatever hole he's fled to. I fling aside the sheet to reveal another tunnel carved out of the rock behind it.

Without hesitation, I launch myself into the dark corridor and run as fast as I dare. It ends quickly at another open airlock and another transparent docking tube attached to it.

Without thinking or worrying about what might be on the other side, I run down the tube. I'm not worried about a random member of Poulter's crew getting away—they're likely to just go to ground and try to join another gang in another system. But if the pirate leader escapes, he'll come back someday for blood, with twice as many men and women to back him up. The future of Carter's World depends on stopping Poulter.

To my relief, the airlock at the other end of the tube is still open wide, and I very quickly find myself inside the Koratan corvette that I guess must be Poulter's flagship of his measly fleet of two. Guessing on instinct and general ship design, I turn left at a junction and run toward where I assume the bridge to be.

I find it a moment later, coming to a skittering halt as I enter the relatively small but open space to find Poulter staring me down along with five other pirates. That's when I remember I still don't have a weapon.

I am so dead.

CHAPTER 26

Ninja Lin

Poulter smiles, though it's more of a disdainful sneer than anything else, and he momentarily reminds me of Petty Officer Nedrin Jacobs, the King's rapist nephew, back on Persephone.

"Well, well, well, if it isn't Captain Brad Mendoza of the Promethean Navy. I've been looking forward to this."

I frown. "Why does *everyone* know who I am in this blasted sector?"

He grins again, showing his teeth, but makes no response. I suddenly have the feeling that this entire time, I've been walking into a trap, though I can't fathom how the pirate leader could know me or know that I was coming.

At a sign from Poulter, a big pirate steps forward, covered in piercings and tattoos, and I recognize the guy as the one who stole my fake wedding ring, credits, and pearls when I posed as a woman on the orbital station. He moves toward me now, wearing a sneer a lot like his boss. I square my shoulders and ready myself to not go down without a fight, but the four other pirates in the room, all except Poulter himself and the guy approaching me, are covering me with their guns now.

My brain is racing, and I can see no path from this that ends with me alive. Still, I don't intend to go quietly, and when the big guy gets within a meter of me, I leap forward and hit him with a jab to the throat.

His hands fly to his neck as he suddenly can't breathe. It's a sucker punch, pure and simple, but I've done real damage to the guy's windpipe, and the scant satisfaction I get from that will have to be the last shred of happiness I get before I die... again. I brace myself for the feel of bullets hitting me; I've never been shot before, but I've heard it really sucks.

Then two things happen in rapid succession. First, Poulter cries out in surprise. Second, a gun barks from behind me, and one of the other pirates drops to the deck.

Then everyone is firing, and I lunge down to the deck next to the guy I just put there. He's gasping for breath and in a real panic, and I'm right there with him now as I can literally *feel* the bullets flying overhead.

Still, I manage to look up to see that just two of the pirates are still standing, plus Poulter, who is crouched behind a console now to one side of the small bridge. I crane my neck to look behind me and spot a completely unexpected figure taking cover behind the edge of the hatchway. Kayla!

She's dressed in the same vacsuit that the militia troops are wearing, and I can only guess she must have disguised herself as one of them and stowed away with them in the *Wanderer's* cargo hold. And now she's trying to have a gunfight with three pirates just to save my sorry rear end.

I've never liked her as much as I do now.

But regardless, she's outmatched and outgunned, though she must be a better shot than I would have expected, given that she's already downed two of the pirates. Even so, if I don't help her now, she's unlikely to get the rest.

I crawl over to the guy still gasping from my punch to his neck and grab the pistol from his waistband. He's turning purple and doesn't even notice. I raise the pistol and am about to fire at the pirate closest to me when the hatch on the other side of the bridge, behind the pirates, starts to swing open. I change my aim to center on that hatch. If more pirates are allowed in, this could get ugly—well, uglier—real fast.

The hatch doesn't open wide, just a small bit, but

a thin person slips through. I'm tightening my finger on the trigger when I recognize Jessica!

Right after I'd killed Owen Thompson and his thug Tucker on that galaxy-forsaken little rock in the Fiori system, I found Jessica safe on *Wanderer*, having already subdued the mercenary Jules with the help—or, at least, without the resistance of—Harris. I've wondered since what that fight must have been like because I've actually never seen Jessica so much as raise a hand in violence unless it was to hit a reticent ship's control console.

But now, my mouth drops open in shock as I see her lunge at one of the two pirates who remain standing and are shooting back at Kayla. Jess delivers a flying kick to the pirate woman's back like something out of a martial arts movie, knocking the pirate forward and causing her to drop her gun in surprise and stumble out from behind the small duty station she's been using as partial cover. I raise the pistol I'm holding and shoot the pirate right through the chest before she can get her feet back under her.

Jessica keeps moving, landing from her kick and using the momentum to pivot and fall forward into a somersault that brings her to her feet right next to the remaining pirate lackey. This guy sees her coming after watching his comrade go down, and he turns to point his pistol at her, but she knocks it out of his grasp with an open-handed slap, then crouches down and extends her leg as she spins, sweeping his feet out from under him. He gives a startled yelp as he falls and hits the deck hard, and the bridge gets suddenly quiet as all gunfire stops.

I want to look behind me and make sure Kayla is OK, but I can't tear my eyes away from my XO, who doesn't let the fallen pirate recover but stomps down hard with the point of her heel right into his chest, knocking the wind out of him, and then follows it up with a kick to his temple that renders him unconscious.

"Drop the gun!" Kayla shouts, and I look to see Poulter has partially risen from his crouch and is starting to point his pistol at me where I still lie on the deck. He scowls but obeys, dropping the gun and raising his hands as he finishes standing up.

He looks at me in disgust. "Really, Mendoza? You're gonna let your women do all the fighting for you?"

I get up from the deck and use the hand not holding the pistol to brush myself off. "Actually, I prefer to exclusively let women fight on my behalf," I tell him. "I'm very progressive that way." I smile at him.

"Now," I say, pointing my own stolen pistol at his gut, "tell me how you know who I am."

He sneers and stays silent. Oh well, that would have been way too easy. Kayla steps up beside me, her assault rifle also pointed at the guy, but a little lower down. What's that old saying? Hell hath no fury like a woman scorned. If Poulter's not careful, he'll lose any chance of bringing little pirate captains into the galaxy one day. His eyes widen when he sees her up close, and it almost seems like something passes between them. Then, to my surprise, the man appears to relax just a bit, though I'm not sure *I* could relax with a gun pointed at my family jewels.

"Brad? You OK?" Jessica asks, and I look over at her. She's barely breathing hard after taking down two very mean-looking pirates. I nod in response to her question. I think that she and I are going to have to have a very long talk about the seemingly hidden fact that she's some kind of ninja or something. To my questioning gaze, she shrugs and says, "Academy martial arts champ, two years straight." Figures. Does she have to be so good at *everything*?

A shot rings out, incredibly loud in my ear, and I whirl to see Poulter crumple to the deck. Then I look at Kayla, who is holding her smoking rifle and walking over to the now-dead pirate captain. She crouches down and comes up with a small revolver in her hand.

"He had a hideaway gun," she said. "I saw him reach for it when he thought we weren't paying attention."

I nod dumbly. Well, there goes my hope of interrogating the guy, but I'm grateful to be alive.

CHAPTER 27

No Prisoners

There are no prisoners. Apparently, every pirate in the base—all thirty-four of them—chose to fight to the death. Unfortunately, we also lost six of our brave militia fighters. Norman takes it harder than I do, but I find myself surprisingly choked up about it as well. Even though I knew it was a likely outcome, I trained and worked with these people for two full weeks, and I feel the weight of personal responsibility for each one of their deaths. I add their names to the list I carry with me in my implant and my head, of every person who has ever died because of a decision I made.

It doesn't help to know that it was the pirates who chose violence. Often rational thought simply can't overcome the emotional response, no matter how hard we try. I honestly hope that never changes. The day I can rationalize someone's death

—even those of my enemies—is a day that I think I'll sink even lower than I already have in life. I may be a mass murderer, but at least I feel terrible about it.

At the end of the day, I still have one more difficult situation to navigate: the ownership of the spoils. There is a wide variety of loot in the pirate base, and there are the two ships, the corvette and the smaller one. President Carter is obviously keen to get his hands on all of it, especially after the economic hardship the pirates have inflicted on his system. But he's also been unable to pay me even what Kayla originally promised.

Then, I remind him that as the military *leader* of the expedition and as the captain of the ship that brought us here, technically, *I* control the disposition of the spoils. He bristles at that, but he finds it hard to argue with thousands of years of interstellar law.

Luckily for him, I'm feeling generous, or maybe just sympathetic to the plight of his planet's citizens. In the end, I keep the corvette, which is what I *really* wanted as soon as I learned of its existence, plus enough loot to cover the operations for it and *Wanderer* for a few months. The rest of the loot, which is pretty substantial, plus the system patrol craft, I let the people of Carter's World have.

I'm such a good guy sometimes. OK, rarely, but I do

have my moments.

Carter's not really happy, but his daughter glares at him when he tries to argue again, and he shuts his mouth.

The biggest question now is what to do given that I have two ships but only two pilots. That means no one to spell either myself or Lin, and that one of us will be alone on a ship while the other will only have Harris for company. I briefly consider asking if any of the militia fighters are interested in a career change, but I stop myself, worried that poaching some of his people might make Carter blow a gasket and try to renege on our deal.

Ultimately, I make Lin and Harris fly the corvette off the rock. Normally, I would be more keen to put myself in danger flying an unknown ship, but the pirates have surprisingly taken great care of it, and we even find the ship's command override code written on a sticky note on the captain's command chair. I guess pirates don't really worry about password security.

But actually, the reason I decide to have Jessica fly the bounty ship is so that I can fly *Wanderer* back to Carter's World with the president and his militia. I don't want them anywhere near my new ship, or my crew, if they decide to take a better deal through force, because I have the distinct impression that Carter—who I've never actually liked—would consider that.

I bid an awkward farewell to Jessica in the central lounge that we've used as a staging area for moving out the recovered loot to each of our ships. Carter and his people will have to make a few trips back in their small in-system shuttle to take ownership of the other pirate ship and get the rest of the spoils. But whatever we can fit in the hold while still making room for the surviving nineteen militia troops is going with us now.

"It was a good plan, Brad," Jessica says.

I nod. "Couldn't have come up with it without you...or Harris," I admit.

She chuckles, though it's a bit strained. "Yeah, that was a surprise. We might have to keep the guy around."

I smile, but it's also forced. "Sure. Well, I guess I'll see you at the jump point after I drop off the kids back at the farm."

"OK, Captain. I'll take a run through the outer system to play with our new ship and hopefully work out any kinks before we try to take her into jump space."

I nod, not knowing what else to do. "Uh, what do you want to call her?"

"Really, you're going to let me name the new ship?" she asks in surprise and her face lights up a bit.

"Well, yeah. Without your ninja skills on the bridge, we wouldn't have her. I was pretty much just lying there helpless before you and Kayla showed up." At the mention of Kayla, Jessica's joy abates. Stupid me.

But she thinks for a moment and then tells me the ship's new name.

"Really?" I ask in genuine surprise.

She nods resolutely. "Really. She did save us in the end, after all."

Then, with a few more awkward words, Jessica is gone, and I'm turning back to the tunnel that will lead me back to my little freighter and another awkward conversation.

CHAPTER 28

The Long Goodbye

I find Kayla, as expected, in the cockpit waiting for me when I get back on Wanderer. Surprisingly, her father and Norman aren't there, which is too bad, because I could really use them as a buffer right now. I can only assume that Carter is resting in his cabin after the ordeal of the day, and Norman is probably still down with his troops in the hold.

"Hey, flyboy," she says with a smile as I slide into the pilot's chair. She's sitting in Jessica's co-pilot chair, which actually bothers me, but I don't say anything.

"Hey back," I say lamely, my mind racing to find words for what I want to say to her.

Neither of us talks as I work to ready the ship. Jessica and Harris already have the corvette burning away from the rock; even though its unfamiliar, warships tend to be faster to warm up and get going than a civilian freighter like *Wanderer*. Kayla lets me work in silence, and fifteen minutes later our landing skids lift gently off the low-gravity surface.

"So, you need a new chief engineer for either of your ships?" Kayla finally asks.

"Uh, I think your father would kill me if I took you away," I say.

She smiles. "Yeah, he probably would. But that doesn't mean I have to listen to what he wants. You and I, we make a great team. At least, *I* think so."

I hesitate in my response, second guessing what I already decided to tell her before even saying my goodbyes to Jessica. "Uh, listen, Kayla, I…"

She surprises me by reaching across and putting a finger to my lips. "Quiet, flyboy. I'm serious about running away from this place with you. Let's go together, right after we drop Dad and his soldiers off, and let's go to a system where they've never even heard of Carter's World, or Gerson, or any of the other places we come from. We'll run cargo, maybe play mercenaries, and hold each other every night. And if you sell that info Walters thinks you have to her or the highest bidder, it'll be all we need to get started in our new lives."

I roll this over in my head for a moment, but not because I'm actually tempted by it. No, something just feels off about her offer. But I can't think what it is, so I just shake my head slowly. "Kayla, I can't."

She nods and smiles sadly, tears forming in her eyes. "I know. You love Jessica Lin. Any fool can see it, and she loves you back; any fool can see that as well." I'm going to argue that point with her, but I wisely hold my tongue.

She gets up, but before she goes, she leans down and kisses me gently, her lips brushing mine as if begging me to reconsider. Then she's gone and I'm alone in the cockpit.

CHAPTER 29

The Revelation

Three hours later, when the corvette with Jessica and Harris on board is almost off my sensor scope, the comm chimes that I have an incoming hail. I answer it.

"Brad, can you hear me?" Jessica's voice asks over the cockpit speakers.

"I can, Jess, what's up?" There's an urgency to her tone that tells me this isn't just a social call.

"Put me on your implant so no one else can listen in," she says next, and my wariness spikes. I get up and close the cockpit door, then do as she says.

"OK, we're good," I say. "Now tell me, what's going on?"

"I don't know," she admits. "I just can't shake the feeling that we missed something. Did that whole mission feel, I don't know, too easy?"

On the surface, it sounds crazy, given all we went through to take out Poulter and his goons, but the same thing has been nagging at me. For all the many things that had to go right for our mission to succeed, it seems like it all went off without a hitch. We should have had at least one hitch—maybe three or four.

"Yeah, I think I know what you mean," I tell her honestly. Then, a thought hits me. "Jessica, what *exactly* did your father do while you were stationed on *Ordney* that makes you hate him so much?"

There's silence on the other end of the line, and I'm worried that maybe I've lost the connection or just lost her by asking the one question she's told me she won't answer.

"Brad..." she starts, but I jump back in.

"I know Jess, but I need you to trust me. I need to know. I can't explain why, but I just need to know right now."

Another long pause. When she starts talking again, her voice is subdued. "I told him where to meet me in the Hothan system, so he knew where *Ordney* was on our patrol. Brad, we were part of the *Intrepid* task force. So, he knew where the *entire* task force was going to be, and, more importantly, where it *wasn't* going to be."

She says the last part like it should hold great meaning for me. At first, it doesn't, but when the realization hits me, it's like a ton of bricks.

"The Yolandra Incident…"

"Yes," she confirms, in a whisper that I have to strain to hear even with my implant's direct connection to my inner ear. "Fifty-seven spacers dead, and a whole shipment of warship components lost."

And not just *any* warship components; these were components that King Charles had somehow managed to procure from a star nation in the Outer Rim, hundreds of light years closer to Earth than the Promethean Federation. Components more advanced than anything out in the Fringe, and that could have changed the whole nature of our cold war with Koratas and put Prometheus into the conversation with star nations like the Leeward Republic as a major player in Fringe power politics.

"They never found out who leaked the fleet's location or even who attacked the convoy," I protest, still disbelieving what she's telling me.

Another long silence follows my statement, but I'm dreading what I'm going to hear next.

"Yes, they did," she says morosely, "on both counts. But Naval Intelligence thought they would use me to keep feeding information—the false information *they* wanted—to my father, and from him, to the Republic."

"He earned your trust and then double-crossed you," I gasp. "He gave you the thing you longed for most, and then used it against you."

And suddenly everything starts to fall into place.

"Jessica, let me call you back," I say before she can say anything else. Then I soften my tone. "And trust me, if anyone in the galaxy understands the guilt you've felt ever since then, it's me. We'll get through it together, I promise. But I have to make a really important call right now and confirm the one last thing for this entire mess to make sense."

"OK. But call back soon. I need to know you're OK, Brad. And be careful!" There's genuine concern in her voice and it warms my heart despite the sinking feeling in my stomach that's getting worse and worse with every new revelation.

I sign off and use my implant's interface with the comm to call another number. After fifteen minutes of making bold requests and subtle threats, I'm finally on the line with an older, gruff-sounding man, whose voice I've definitely never heard before.

"This is President Carter. Who is this?"

"Mr. President, this is the man who just saved your system from Poulter and his pirates."

"What? You did? We wondered about that ship that snuck out there. Was that you?"

"Yes, but I need you to stop asking questions right now and answer one of mine. Please."

Silence, so I forge ahead. "Do you have a daughter?"

"Yes," he says, though his voice is now filled with hostility and suspicion, "and if you even think about—"

"Please, Mr. President," I cut him off, though I already know the answer, at least partially, to what I'm about to ask next. "I mean her and the rest of your family and your people no harm. But I need to know; how old is she?"

A long pause. "Forty-two. She's married with her own kids these days. Why?"

"I can't explain. Only in a little while, you're probably going to get a call from someone named Jessica Lin, or possibly Jennifer Kim—she goes by both. She's with me, and I need you to promise that you'll do whatever she asks to help her. Do it in return for us liberating your system. Got it?"

"I don't know what you're babbling about, son, but if she calls, I'll listen."

"Thank you, Mr. President."

I cut the line and start to hail the corvette and Jessica again. But before I can finish, I hear the hatch behind me slam open, and then I feel the cold steel of a pistol's muzzle pressed to the back of my neck.

"Tsk, tsk, tsk," Kayla's voice says, though in a slightly lower register than before. "Now, Brad, you hurt my feelings once already today. Let's not make things any worse."

I turn slowly in my seat, mindful of the gun and keeping my hands where she can see them and look at the pretty little farm girl. Though she's no longer pretty or a farm girl. Her face is curled into a sneer, and she's wearing a black skinsuit with ballistic armor attached. On top of that, she holds the pistol like an extension of her arm.

"Kayla, or whatever your name is, just tell me what you want."

She rolls her eyes. "Come on, Brad, even you can't be *that* dense. I've told you already, several times. I want that secret in your head. I want the coordinates of that stellarium deposit out in Gerson."

Crap. So much for hoping she was just going off the little Admiral Walters may have told her, though I still don't know for sure if Walters was in on this or just a dupe like me; either way seems equally likely. It wouldn't surprise me that little Kayla has been ahead of me *and* the admiral this entire time.

"My name *is* Kayla, just not Carter. And you knew a cousin of mine, Jules," she growls, her voice hard and menacing. "In fact, I think you were the last person to see her alive, and I owe you for that."

I want to hit myself in frustration at my own stupidity. I'd left Jules, Owen Thompson's henchwoman, on the surface of that asteroid at Fiori tied up but with a long-range portable comm. I'd done it so that Jessica wouldn't know that I expected Agent of the King's Cross Heather Kilgore to quickly find and kill the mercenary, but I should have at *least* disabled the comm. Apparently, the mean little woman got off at least one call before she met her end.

Now I'm positive that not even Walters knew what she was getting into when she set us up on this job with Kayla. Because Jules knew what Owen was after on that rock—the exact coordinates of the stellarium deposit at Gerson—and Walters would have *never* let me off her ship if she'd suspected I had that bouncing around in my head.

"And Poulter and his pirates?" I ask, though I already know the answer to that as well.

She shrugs. "We made a deal with him: help us get the info out of you and get a cut. They'd setup here in the Carter System as a convenient out-of-the-way base for raids in the Jutzen Protectorate.

"But you ruined everything! You were supposed to just surrender at Big Ben, or at least stay in the atmosphere long enough for Poulter's second ship to arrive and box you in. But you had to go and be all daring, so I had to call them off before you got us killed. Then we had to throw together the little operation at the farm on the fly and call in a bunch more of our team to play the roles of the militia because you just wouldn't give up or give sweet little me the information so we could run off together. You're a very annoying mark, Brad."

She grins wickedly. "But at least you helped us get rid of some troublesome business partners. Poulter kept pushing for a bigger cut of the prize when we finally sold those coordinates in your head. Now, my team and I will get to keep it all to ourselves. So maybe you're not worthless after all."

"Listen," I try to say in a reasonable tone, though I'm pretty annoyed. Why do the villains always insist on monologuing? I'm also, if I'm honest, more than a tiny bit terrified right now. "No one needs to get hurt. I'll share what I know, just let my crew go in peace."

Kayla sneers at me again, showing her teeth, and then looses a wicked laugh. "Sorry, flyboy," for a second, her voice goes back to the soft soprano she used as Kayla Carter, "I can't bear the thought of sharing your affections." Then her voice hardens again. "And I'm afraid I can't have your little trollop coming after us."

I turn back to my console in horror just in time to see the distant sensor reading of the corvette explode. Before I can even process what's happened, rage takes me, and I leap out of my seat with my hands outstretched as claws toward Kayla's throat.

The stun round hits me in the chest, and my world goes black before I even get halfway there.

EPILOGUE

Jessica Lin; Another Death

The fire burns hot and bright, quickly consuming the oxygen around me. I can't breathe, for every time I try my lungs feel nothing but searing pain and heat. When I cough, the agony is so intense that I wish for all the universe to be dead, but I'm sure I already am.
"Jessica! Jessica!" a faint but frantic voice screams, and it takes me a second to recognize its owner.

Harris? What is he doing here in Hades with me? I always liked him. Too bad he had to join me in Hell.

"Jessica! You're alive!" That can't be right. He's delusional. Poor Harris; unlike me, he's never been dead before.

Something heavy comes off my chest, and I feel something soft press to my face. Cool air suddenly replaces the hot fires of perdition that have been scorching my lungs, and I gulp in great ragged breaths, desperately grateful for even the momentary reprieve.

"I think the ship is still flyable," Harris is saying, though I don't know quite what he's talking about.

"Just hold on, Jessica. They have Brad. We have to go after them!"

Brad. Brad. Brad. The name takes up in my mind like a drum beat, over and over again in time with the throbbing of the pain that still pulses through my body in agonizing waves.

Brad. I grasp onto the word and use it to fight my way up out of the dark fires that grasp me. My eyes fly open and I see Harris' face staring down at me through a haze that slowly resolves into smoke. He looks worried.

"Brad?" I ask, but the sound leaves my ragged lungs and lips in a mangled groan that is further muffled by whatever is on my face.

"They have him, Jessica. They have the captain. You need to live so we can go after him. They have the captain." He's frantically jabbering now, and part of me wants to reach out and slap him, but it's too painful for me to move my arm.

"Hold on, Jessica!" he pleads. "I'll get you to the auto-doc. The burns are so bad. Just stay with me for a few more minutes, please!"

I close my eyes as I feel him struggle to lift me from the hard deck of...the ship. *Persephone.* But that ship's destroyed… No. It must be our new ship, the one we took from…pirates? That's right. I told Brad I wanted to call her *Persephone*. Like the other ship…like…

"Brad!" I scream as my eyes fly open. But the pain is too much as Harris jolts and jars my body while he rushes down the corridor, and I feel blessed oblivion coming back to claim me.

But right before unconsciousness washes over me, I have one last desperate thought.

Brad, I'm coming!

THE END OF BOOK THREE

NOTE TO THE READER

I wrote four different endings and six different epilogues to this installment before I settled on what you've just read. And it really came down to one thing: I've been hesitant to write from the standpoint of Jessica Lin. My first draft of Book Two—what eventually became *The Worst Spies in the Sector*—had every other chapter written from Jessica's point of view. I ultimately abandoned that because how could I, as a man, possibly write her innermost thoughts after all she's been through? So instead, I chose to keep that book and most of this one from Brad's point of view.

But, as I wrote this third book, it kept coming back to Jessica. It's seems impossible to properly explore her awesome character if we're limited to just Brad's point of view. So, Book Four, *The Worst Rescuers in the Republic,* which is already partially written, will feature portions of the story as seen through both their eyes. I hope I can do Jessica justice.

I've gotten a lot of reviews and comments on social

media asking me to keep this series going for a long time. I love hearing that from my readers, and I promise I've taken it to heart. Book Four won't be the end of this story, not by a long shot. I often say that my characters tend to write themselves, and Brad and Jessica have a *lot* of adventures left in them that are begging to be told. So, sit back and enjoy the ride. It's going to be a wild one!

BOOKS BY SKYLER RAMIREZ

Dumb Luck & Dead Heroes

The Worst Ship in the Fleet

The Worst Spies in the Sector

The Worst Pirate Hunters in the Fringe

The Worst Rescuers in the Republic (coming early 2024!)

The Four Worlds

The Four Worlds: The Truth

The Four Worlds: Subversion

Revolution: A Four Worlds Story (coming early 2024!)

ABOUT THE AUTHOR

Skyler S. Ramirez

 Mr. Ramirez writes science fiction and fantasy that entertains, thrills, uplifts, and inspires. His books contain surprising plot twists that keep you guessing, exciting universes that fuel the imagination, and thought-provoking drama that keeps you coming back for more. But at the end of the day, all of his writing centers around one theme: how relatively ordinary men and women can do extraordinary things. As a student of history, he believes this to be true and loves exploring the motivations and deeply held beliefs and dreams of his characters.

Skyler writes books that adults will enjoy but that he wouldn't be embarrassed or worried for his teenage children to read. He feels that great stories don't need foul language, graphic scenes, or other window dressing to make them exciting. A good story stands on its own.

Mr. Ramirez lives with his wife, Lindsey, and their four children in Texas. When he is not writing, he has been and continues to be a leader and executive with multiple Fortune 500 and Fortune 1000 companies.

He would love it if you subscribed to his newsletter, which you can do at https://www.skylerramirez.com/join-the-club.

Made in United States
Orlando, FL
01 March 2024

44287079R00098